THE
BARTER TRADE
A NOVEL

CHRIS RUFFLE

The Barter Trade

By Chris Ruffle

ISBN-13: 978-988-8843-73-2

FICTION

EB215

Published in Hong Kong by Earnshaw Books Ltd.

Also by Chris Ruffle:

A Decent Bottle of Wine in China

CHAPTER ONE
First Sight

He checked the number on the plywood door. Twenty-one. On the second floor of the dreaded Erligou negotiation building. He checked his watch. 10:00 a.m. More or less. Punctuality was not a big deal here. He checked his tie and shirt front—only a couple of wrinkles and a small spot of breakfast jam. Smart business attire was not a big thing here either. He knocked.

Deng yi huir! a woman shouted from inside. "Wait a moment!" The Peking accent, with an emphasis on the rolling 'r', was slight but noticeable. Ben had spent only two months in Peking—or Beijing, as it was properly called, "the Northern Capital". He had already done a lot of waiting, so had no difficulty recognizing this particular phrase.

Hao. Qing jin! He went in, as instructed, opening the door carefully, unsure of what he would find. There was just one young woman, filling the last of six tea mugs, each fitted with a lid to keep the liquid warm. The mugs, an indispensable component of any Chinese meeting, were lined up, three on each side of the long table.

"Is this the place for the meeting with Section Manager Zhang?" he asked in Chinese. He had studied Chinese at college back in England, picking the most obscure course he could find on the Universities and Colleges Admissions Course's (UCAS) form in an act of rebellion designed to upset his parents. So he was able to handle conversations, as long as they kept within the tram lines of common usage.

"Yes, that's right" she said. "But I thought there were to be three of you? Where is the rest of your delegation?"

"Oh, they went to the washroom. They'll be here in a moment."

He smiled. His "delegation" was one overweight Mancunian and a rather dour, jet-lagged Glaswegian.

"Well, please sit down." He sat down in the farthest seat, leaving the central seat for his delegation leader, the Mancunian. "Section Manager Zhang will be here shortly." She sat down opposite, picking a notepad and biro from her bag. There was an awkward silence.

"The weather's very cold" he said. Everyone was back from their Chinese New Year holidays, so earlier they had waited half an hour for a taxi at the hotel. Inside the taxi, a copy of an old Soviet model badged 'Shanghai,' it was colder than outside. "The heater isn't working," the heavily muffled driver said, stating the obvious and taking a swig from a jam jar full of tea leaves. The jar was jammed into the gap next to the parking brake, wrapped in a flannel which proved to have several functions. Not only did it insulate the tea but could also be employed to wipe the driver's neck and de-mist the fogged-up front window.

"Yes, my bicycle was frosted this morning." "Have you far to cycle?"

"No, my parent's house is, fortunately, not too far away." She smiled back. She was slim with short, bobbed black hair. She wore no make-up, but then no women did here. There was a mole above her right eye. Bright pink long-johns, clearly worn for warmth rather than fashion, were visible between her trousers cuffs and plimsolls.

There was a tentative rap on the door, it opened and a large bespectacled head with an impressive comb-over peered around it. "Ah, here we are," said Timothy Vowles, export director of Consarc Ltd., manoeuvring his bulk around the door and onto a chair that had not been designed to handle it. He smiled at the girl and, while lowering himself, whispering to Ben, "It was one of those long-drop toilets. Hard to balance. And no paper. I had to use one of my brochures."

Alex Gordon, Consarc's technical director, folded himself into the third chair. He did not smile but sucked his teeth and furrowed thick eyebrows.

"Pleased to meet you," said Vowles, speaking especially slowly, while rummaging in his briefcase for his recently printed name cards. He was proud that they had a Chinese translation on the reverse side. "I'm…"

"I will let Section Manager Zhang know you are here," the girl interrupted in good English, leaving the room.

"Are you okay?" Ben asked when she had left, showing professional concern. Consarc was one of the larger clients of Oremin, the trading company for which he worked.

"It must have been something I ate on the plane. My stomach hasn't been great since I arrived."

"Don't worry. I've got a whole range of cement tablets when we get back to the office." Vowles looked puzzled. "You know, to solidify things down there… So if you could just hold on for a while."

"Needs must."

"I told him not to eat it," frowned Gordon, shaking his head at his colleague's folly.

"Drink some tea," Ben said, gesturing to the mugs on the table, which the girl had just filled. Vowles lifted the mug lid tentatively and took an experimental slurp, completely filling his mouth with the tea leaves which floated on the surface. He spat the offending material back into the cup and spluttered "How do you avoid the tea leaves?"

"You need to blow before you suck."

Vowles wiggled his eyebrows suggestively. "I bet you say that to all the girls!"

At the second slurp, the assistant re-entered with, presumably, Section Manager Zhang, as well as a younger man. Both were in well-worn blue Mao jackets. They moved to the other side of the table. Zhang, taking the center seat, gave a small bow and presented his name card to Vowles. "*Huanying dao Beijing*," he said. "Welcome to Beijing," the girl translated. Zhang then handed name cards to Gordon and Ben.

The cards carried the logo of CMIEC, the China Machinery Import Export Corporation, one of the larger government agencies that handled international trade. The younger man turned out to be Deputy Section Manager Lin. Everyone exchanged cards. The office had come up with nice-sounding translations of the English names rather than simple transliterations. Vowles became Wei. Gordon became Gao, which, appropriately, meant 'tall'. The company had become Kangsai or 'Resist Competition.' The girl's card said her surname was Peng.

As the visitors resettled themselves, Ben said, in Chinese, "Thank you for taking the time to see us today. As this is our first meeting, perhaps Manager Wei can first make a brief introduction of our company and its products?"

"That would be good" said Zhang. As the section manager stretched his legs under the table, Ben noticed he favored the same style long-johns as Miss Peng, only these were in a fetching turquoise. "You're on," Ben whispered to Vowles, who started his spiel, with Ben translating. Ben had read through the material and had held a short discussion over dinner the previous evening, so he did not make too big a hash of the vocabulary. On a couple of terms, Miss Peng, clearly a more experienced interpreter, gently corrected him.

The discussion took in mass spectroscopy and its use to determine the molecular weight and structure of peptides and proteins based on the ionization and fragmentation of sample molecules in the gas phase. There were enough intelligent questions from Messrs Zhang and Lin to indicate that Consarc was not wasting its time in seeking to develop the China market. Vowles proudly revealed the company was planning to exhibit its top-of-the-range mass spectrometer at an equipment exhibition in Shanghai in the following month and hoped that Zhang and colleagues could attend.

Zhang inquired how long the delegation intended to stay in Beijing. When he was told Friday, he suggested dinner on Thursday, as there was a work unit, a drug producer that might like to attend and learn more. Agreed, hands were shaken. Miss Peng said she would call Ben at the office to confirm the time and place for dinner. The visitors headed back to the office and, for Vowles, a cement tablet and a proper sit-down toilet with a plentiful supply of paper.

Chapter Two
Miss Peng's Diary (translation)

I really didn't feel up to it this morning. I have only been back at my work unit for a few days after New Year's, and my mind is still in holiday mode. Yesterday's article on the new Labor Contract law was one reason to go into work. Another was my colleague Meiyu, who'd wangled a business trip to Japan. When will I get a chance? I am not asking for much — perhaps this new law will cause those in charge to appreciate my hard work. Anyway, I don't envy Meiyu going to Japan, because I am going to get to the UK, where they are gentlemen, like the newly arrived Englishman who came to the office today. He thinks his Chinese is good, when it is only so-so. But he has nice curly hair, a big nose and thin lips. He was very polite and thanked everybody. Perhaps he will bring an opportunity for me this year. Aunty is always worrying me about when I will find a husband. At the dinner table at New Year, everyone in the family was going on about what they had achieved. Perhaps I will be this year's dark horse and people will appreciate what I have done? So let's not worry about little old Japan. With the weather here so bright and cold, my hands are freezing and I need to warm them up on my hot water bottle. Let's see if these hands are strong enough to catch a foreign dream.

1983.3.4 阳历

今天真是没劲，年后回到单位没多少天，心♥裡还想著大年夜大伙在一起的日子，要不是为了咋人民日报上的劳动合同法，我还不想上工呢☹。特别又要再次面对对门的美玉，她马上就要去日本出差了，而我那年呢???????……本来就不想吃大锅饭过日子，现在新法应该可以让胡主任看到我的能力，一点都不输美玉，谁要去小日本呢，我可要去大英国，那里的人才绅士呢，不像小

↓人生图一个洋鬼子梦！

7

CHAPTER THREE
Banquet

"Do I *really* have to drink more of this?" Vowles complained, *sotto voce*.

They were having a dinner with CMIEC as arranged, in a private room at one of the capital's roast duck restaurants. This one was located near a major hospital, so some wit had dubbed it the 'Sick Duck' restaurant. There were eight around the table. It was only 6:10 p.m. but the revolving lazy Susan in the center was already groaning with food. Vowles was seated on Section Chief Zhang's right, and Gordon was to his left, next to Miss Peng, who was helping with interpretation, as Ben was doing on the other side. The rest of the table was made up of Deputy Chief Lin, a man and woman from the Shanghai No.5 Special Chemical Works and someone Ben had mentally tabbed as 'the Drinker'. His sole role seemed to be to eat and propose toasts to the foreigners to try to get them well oiled.

"You look a bit of a wimp if you don't knock it back," Ben whispered. "Just make sure everybody else drinks at the same time. If they all start toasting you individually, you will be in big trouble."

"What's it made of?" "Sorghum. A kind of. 'Millet'.

"That really doesn't help me. I had it down as a hydrocarbon derivative…"

Zhang once again raised his tiny glass of the colourless but potent liquid. "I would like to welcome Mr Vowles and Gordon to China." Miss Peng translated. "I hope that this marks the start of a long cooperation which will be of mutual benefit to both our countries. *Ganbei*!" Zhang drained the glass, theatrically tipping it upside down to show that all the liquor was gone. The rest of the table followed suit. Vowles winced as the *Moutai* went down, then immediately reached for a glass of the non-alcoholic alternative for dilution. Unfortunately, that alternative was a fizzy orange juice that had never seen an orange. Its taste reflected its industrial origins.

"Are you originally from Beijing, Mr Zhang?"

"No, from the Northeast. But I came as a student and have worked here for over fifteen years now, so I count at least as half a Beijinger."

"Oh, that must have been during the Cultural Revolution?" blurted Vowles. Ben kicked him under the table.

"Yes, there was a big movement of people around the country at that time. I see you have been reading our history, Mr Vowles."

"No, we were just talking about it last night. How things are changing. Deng Xiaoping's 'Open Door Policy and all that. Do you have children?" Vowles unskilfully changed the topic of conversation.

"Just one. A son. He's about to go to college.'

"Oh, what will he be studying?"

"Mechanical engineering".

"Good choice. Smart boy." The conversation then meandered along the normal, safer channel of families, travel, impressions of China and views on Chinese food:

"Oh, this is all absolutely delicious," said Vowles, smacking his lips to add authenticity. "This… er… dish is particularly tasty." When the focus of attention shifted to Gordon, who was fielding questions from the pharmaceutical couple, Vowles leaned over and, gesturing to his plate, whispered to Ben: "What is this exactly?"

"It is best not to ask. You might not like the answer."

"But what is it?"

"Bat soup. I would give it a wide berth, myself."

"Fair enough".

Vowles failed to repress a shudder. Looking for re-assurance, he said, "This one over here tastes Okay, Just like chicken."

"It is chicken."

"Ah! That would explain it."

At this point, the Drinker lurched forward and proposed a toast to Messrs Vowles and Gordon of everlasting mutual friendship between their great nations. Miss Peng translated, giving a wry smile in acknowledgment that the Drinker had already given the same toast earlier in the meal.

Miss Peng was confining herself to the orange drink — because of her sex, she was given a pass on rocket-fuel consumption. Lucky her. Ben smiled and toasted her back in orange juice. Zhang leaned over, and using his own chopsticks, helped Vowles to another sea slug.

"Oh, thank you very much". Once Zhang's attention moved in the other direction, Vowles carefully tucked the slimy, pimpled sea slug under a pile of cabbage on the plate's edge. Turning to Ben, he whispered "They like eating these? Really?"

"Oh, they're terribly good for you. And they can't afford them on their own salaries, so when they're entertaining honoured foreign guests at the state's expense..."

"Well, it's not going to catch on in Stockport. 'Two sea slugs and chips, please, Love.' "

He tittered. "Do you think now would be a good time to

introduce this?" Vowles indicated his bag below the table, from which a bottle of Scottish whisky was protruding.

"Isn't that a bit dangerous? In terms of mixing drinks, I mean." At least they were close to a hospital. "We've got a long train journey ahead, so you might want to hang on to it."

"Gordon's got another." Turning to his host, Vowles produced the bottle, like a magician from a hat. "Mr Zhang, this is a drink I have brought from my home country." The drinker at the end of the table, smiled and bent forward, his professional interest piqued for the first time that evening.

After that, the dinner got a little messy, but still finished exactly on the two-hour mark. All official dinners lasted two hours. It concluded in a fug of smiles, cigarette smoke and back-slapping. CMIEC's client, the drug makers, seemed happy at what they had heard and promised to attend next month's exhibition in Shanghai, where they could examine a sample of the type of spectrometer in which they were most interested.

As coats were collected and a taxi called, Ben had a chance for a brief chat with Miss Peng. She was a recent graduate from the electrical department of prestigious Fudan University in Shanghai. Her particular interest was the new field of personal computing. "But it is so difficult to get any time on one, or to be able to read the latest articles," she said.

Ben saw his chance. "But I've got a PC in my room," he boasted. It was a tiny Sinclair ZX Spectrum, which he used to play games when bored. "When you have time, you are most welcome to come to try it out. Perhaps at the weekend?"

CHAPTER FOUR
Home from Home

Ben had lived, since his arrival, at the inappropriately named Friendship Hotel. It was a compound of twelve Soviet-style gray blocks constructed at what, in 1983, was the far north western corner of Beijing, in the direction of the Fragrant Hills and the Summer Palace. It housed an odd mixture of 'foreign experts' and political refugees—a Scandinavian metallurgist here, the former head of the Ugandan Marxist party there. Any Chinese attempting to enter the compound was questioned by the guards at the gate about why they were visiting All foreigners lived in hotels, apart from diplomats, who were lodged in a comfortable but closely monitored apartment complex downtown, together with foreign journalists, who were similarly regarded as spies.

Ben's accommodation, room 1450, was acceptable if a little drab. There were two rooms—a lounge and a bedroom. The radiators worked, though they sounded like a euphonium being tuned up.

There was a metal hot-water flask, which was refilled regularly. Packets of green tea came gratis. There was little decoration but a Tang three-color ceramic horse which Ben had bought for twenty-five yuan (the official exchange rate was three yuan to one pound). He had probably been ripped off, but thought it would make a good present for his Mum when he next got home.

Ben had brought in a tape recorder with him. Most of his luggage was made up of music tapes and reading—he favored Russian epics and Victorian novels as offering the best weight-to-reading-time ratio. There was no reason to turn on the TV—the programmes were dire, consisting almost entirely of propaganda, Beijing operas or documentaries about tractor production. So Ben had rigged it up as the screen for his ZX Spectrum. He spent quite a lot of time writing letters home.

The food in the hotel was nourishing if dull. In winter, Beijing offered only two kinds of vegetables, *bai cai* or *you cai*; that is to say, cabbage or cabbage. Ben had already learnt eight different words for what was essentially cabbage—for an Englishman at least. Fruit that came from the south, such as oranges, arrived in the capital wizened and scarred, so local apples were a better bet. The hotel restaurant did offer some Western dishes, but these were best avoided. The hardest meal to stomach was breakfast. China's five thousand years of civilization had resulted in a breakfast that consisted of rice gruel with pickled vegetables. Even for a man as open-minded as Ben thought himself, pickled vegetables were hard to take at seven in the morning. So he persisted with the treacly coffee and cold toast smeared with an unidentified fruit jam. The highlight was a drinkable yoghurt in small glass bottles. Many Chinese were lactose-intolerant, so yoghurt seemed to be the main dairy product available.

Miss Peng had said she would come over on Sunday afternoon. Ben was a little worried about the guards, so was expecting a call from the front gate. Instead there was a tap at the door. He jumped up to open it. "Come in, come in." She stood swaddled in a thick, blue padded jacket. "Make yourself warm. It's warmest over here by the radiator. Would you like some tea?"

Underneath she was wearing a patterned dress, worn with the same luminous long johns as when they had first met at Erligou. "You didn't have any problem at the gate? I was a little worried."

"No. I have my business card. My job is dealing with foreign businessmen so... my visit will, of course, be reported to my work unit, but that should not be a problem."

"Well, it's lovely to see you. Here. Sit down. Drink some tea ."

They sat and chatted in a mixture of Chinese and English. Mostly English. Her father had what sounded like a fairly senior role in the shipbuilding ministry. Her mother was a teacher. There was a younger sister. Ben responded, telling her how he had ended up in Beijing. "But this is what you wanted to see." He enthusiastically introduced his computer, the ZX Spectrum with Microdrive.

She wasn't quite sure what to make of it at first. She turned over the small black keyboard with the little rainbow stripe at the corner. They played some games — Ant Attack, Manic Miner and Donkey Kong. She was competitive. When she was concentrating, she had the unconscious habit of sticking the tip of her tongue out between her teeth. When excited, she would rub her hands together. She talked about her time at college, and they compared notes. Her course at Fudan sounded more formal than Ben's undergraduate studies back in England; teachers talked, the students wrote down what they said, then regurgitated it at exam time. Student feedback was not encouraged. On graduation, it was the university that had assigned her a job. She had done well to be assigned back to Beijing. Her *hukou*, an internal passport designed to limit the flow of farmers into big cities, was from Beijing, after all. Students who fell afoul of their professor could easily end up in Xinjiang, from where it could be a long road home.

When it reached 5:00 p.m. he asked her whether she would

like to get something to eat at the hotel. In China, dinner was early. If you did not eat by seven then you were going to go hungry. But she needed to get back, she said — her parents would be expecting her. Perhaps they could meet up again? She said there was no phone at home, so best to call the office. He had her card with the number and extension. She wrapped herself up again and waved as she strode away down the under-lit corridor.

CHAPTER FIVE
Diary 23/2/83

I had the chance to use an eight-bit computer called 'Spectrum' today. It had been imported by an Englishman staying at the Friendship Hotel. The keyboard is spongy and hard to use, but I was still able to type faster than he. He was friendly. He said to call him Ben and joked that this can mean 'stupid' in Chinese if pronounced with the fourth tone, so I needed to say his name with care. It was a good chance to practice my non-business English vocabulary. At dinner I told Pa and Ma I had been working, which was partly the truth.

```
1. YOUR LETTERE COME THROUGH REGULARLY AND TAKE ABOUT 6
DAYS.

2. OXFORD BEAT CAMBRIDGE IN BOAT RACE BY MANY LENGTHS.

3. CORRECTION:  GRAND NATIONAL ON APRIL9TH.   WILL SELECT A/A
BACK ONE FOR YOU.

4. BONAR BRENTFORD BEST SELECTION FOR TRANSFORMERS.   HAVE ASKED
AS ALTERNATIVE A BELGIUM COMPANY PAUWELES OF MECHELEN TO CONTACT YOU
IF INTERESTED.   REQUIRE MORE INFORMATION FROM YOU ON CHLOROPRENE
RUBBER.   IS IT A FACTORY EQUIPMENT OR FOR APPLYING THE MATERIALS
IF YOU CAN OBLIGE THE MACHINERY EDITOR OF PLASTICS AND RUBBER
WEEKLY WILL FIND FOR YOU.   HAVE YOU GOT PRICE RIGHT IN YOUR
TELEX

5. INFORMATION ON KRR RECORDING STUDIO WELL RECEIVED.

6.  SHALL BE SENDING BOOKS AND TAPES VIA TIM VOWLES OF AE (EXPORT
SERVICES) WHO IS VISITING YOU ABOUT APRIL 20TH

7. GOOD LUCK WITH SHANGHAI EXHIBITION


LOVE DAD
```

Chapter Six
The Office

Ben's office was a suite of rooms in another hotel. This hotel, near the Beijing Zoo, was so filled with the representative offices of foreign companies that it had lost its original function. Its only claim to fame was the Moscow Restaurant, set up when relations with the Soviet Union were still warm. It still served Russian dishes and was probably the only restaurant in the world where it was possible to slurp borscht while watching an elephant.

Each day, Ben got a lift to work with the Cantonese couple for whom he worked. The couple, both from Hong Kong, also lived at the Friendship. They could have got a taxi, but the supply was unreliable, so the company had invested in its own car. When Ben strolled over, Yu was proudly dusting off his car with a brush made of brown cock feathers. This initially seemed odd to Ben, but, as he was discovering, it rarely rained in Beijing but it was very dusty; according to that font of unreliable statistics, the China Daily, dust falls in the capital at a rate of thirty tonnes per square kilometer. So cocktails seemed to do the job.

Yu was tall and quiet. His wife, Shirley, was short, loud and pregnant. Lung power was useful when dealing with the decrepit Chinese telephone system, which made for a noisy work environment, especially as they all sat around two desks which had been pushed together in the center of what was once a hotel bedroom. *"Wei! Wei!"* the Chinese all-purpose phone greeting, was shouted at high volume, neck muscles straining, while gripping the Bakelite receiver tightly. Hard as it is to imagine, this is business before the age of mobile phones, internet or PCs (the Spectrum did not serve any practical purpose in this regard). So unreliable phones and a pretty ordinary postal system were the main means of communication, together with the telex. For readers under sixty, this was a machine like a large typewriter where you would first punch out a tape with your message, then feed the tape into the machine for transmission. The telex installed at the Beijing Exhibition Hotel was a "Goldfish" brand. The time and cost of this procedure encouraged abbreviation, from which Ben's English never really rcvrd.

The evening telex back to London, sent at around 5:30, was a fixed pole in the daily schedule. It would list any important developments—the Chinese were bidding for or offering what materials in what size and at what price. Ben quickly became versed in the periodic table and the abbreviated names for metals and chemicals: Zn, Al and V2O5, not zinc, aluminium and vanadium pentoxide. He became familiar with trading terms: CIF (cost insurance freight, i.e. delivered) and FOB (free on board—the buyer pays for freight). L/C thirty days (letter of credit where the seller would be paid within thirty days of presenting documents). CoD (cash on delivery).

Days were not especially intense, but the requirements of business entertainment and travel meant they could be long. They had a modest number of visitors—mostly agency clients or potential customers—but they went through a lot of tea. Much of the work was administrative, sorting out travel arrangements and meeting schedules for incoming delegations of foreign businessmen or outbound Chinese ones. Finding hotel rooms in

Beijing was a nightmare, and the office sofa was regularly called into use.

Marketing in China was relatively concentrated. All foreign trade went through big import/export corporations: Minmetals for the metals industry, Sinochem for chemicals, CMIEC for machinery, and so on. There were provincial branches and some overlap in responsibilities, but the number of key accounts to cover was manageable. The main obstacle to trade was the currency, the renminbi, which was not convertible. So if a factory wanted to import some equipment or materials, they first had to secure an allocation of foreign exchange to cover it. Similarly, if they exported any goods, the foreign exchange had to be handed over to the People's Bank once received. Often the final end-user or supplier was hidden from the foreign counterparty, at least initially. The main place to meet the actual end-users was at exhibitions.

Peking,
27ᵉ March.

北京展览馆饭店用笺

Dear All,

Everytime I write now it seems as though I'm about to go off somewhere — today at noon its Szechwan. I hope you got my letter from Guilin — I should imagine it would take longer to get to Bradford from the outback. Anyway, after posting it, I seem to spend most of my time waiting at airpor

CHAPTER SEVEN
The Assignation

Ben called Haiyan—Miss Peng—at CMIEC a few times when his colleagues were out of the office. Haiyan, her given name, meant 'sea swallow'. He called once on Monday, once on Tuesday and once on Wednesday to be finally told Miss Peng Haiyan was absent. He left a message with her colleague for her to call him back. There was no reply. Until late on Friday:

"Hello."

"Oh, Haiyan. Hello! Thanks for calling back. I was just calling to see if you'd like to come over on Sunday?"

"It would be best to meet outside, somewhere."

"OK, but they say there may be snow this weekend, so..."

"Do you know Purple Bamboo Park?"

"Yes, but it will be quite..."

"There is a bridge near the west entrance. I will meet you under there at 10:00 a.m."

"OK. But it might be better if..."

"See you there. Bye."

It was cold under the bridge. He had cycled there. He had recently bought a bicycle with the unpromising brand name of "Iron Anchor", but it worked. He had arrived a little early, anxious to find the meeting spot, and stood looking at the frozen lake. It was one of those Beijing days when the pollution could have been filtered with a tennis racquet. The prevailing colour of the park was a yellowish-gray. The only green to be seen were a few stunted, dusty pine trees. There were no birds. The only people were a group of old ladies undertaking their calisthenics. They had lined up facing each other, so that the daily exercise could be combined with a catch-up on gossip. The park might be a pleasant place in summer, but it was rather bleak now. He shivered and stamped his boots to keep the blood circulating.

"Hello". She had approached silently from behind.

"Oh, hello! You made me jump. I was feeling like a spy—James Bond—meeting under a park bridge," he smiled. She didn't.

"I am sorry to get you out here."

"It's fine. It only took me fifteen minutes on my trusty bicycle" he gestured at the Iron Anchor, which had fallen over since he had propped it against a fence.

"It's just that, the hotel guard reported to my work unit on my Sunday visit to see you. They told me that it was not appropriate for me to visit you there."

"I'm sorry. I thought, working in foreign trade, you said it would be okay."

"They said I should not see you again. That you are a counter-revolutionary element."

He laughed. "Well, I have heard some brush-off lines in my time, but that takes the biscuit."

Again, she did not smile. He back-pedalled. "I'm sorry if I got you into trouble. Is there anything I can do?"

"I'm not sure. There is my father, but I didn't want to involve him. I think we just need to take care. Shall we walk?"

So they walked. And talked.

She gradually warmed up, despite the chilly atmosphere.

She even smiled at one or two of his weak jokes. By the end of one circumnavigation of the park, they had decided to meet to see a movie the following Saturday. There was a film starring an actress she liked, Pan Hong, set in wartime Chongqing. He learned that her father had been sent to Sichuan during the Cultural Revolution while her mother and sister had gone to Hunan. Only she had been able to stay in Beijing, with an aunt.

"What shall I call you?" asked Ben. "Miss Peng sounds terribly formal."

"Xiao Peng, Little Peng, would be fine. And I can call you Da Ben."

"Oh, 'Big Stupid'. That's very nice!" He pretended to sulk.

She laughed.

"I'd better get back for lunch. See you next Saturday, Big Stupid."

That agreed, they parted. Having found his bike, he cycled back by the longer route, throwing off, in his imagination, the secret agents that were tracking him.

Chapter Eight
TGIF

This week's TGIF was to be held at the New Zealand embassy. Each Friday evening Beijing's small population of resident Westerners would assemble at one of the embassies, to catch up and decide what to do at the weekend. Ben had heard that the Kiwis gave the best parties, so he had been looking forward to it all day.

The "Thank God It's Friday" concept was not entirely appropriate as most private foreign companies still worked on Saturday mornings, just like the Chinese. But the sense of relief, at being able to unburden oneself in sympathetic company, was welcome.

The main tone of conversation was one of complaint — complaints about the difficulties and dangers of the traffic, complaints about contracts and promises broken, complaints about equipment breaking or stuff going missing and the difficulties of putting it right. As the booze flowed (Sauvignon Blanc was a particular treat) and canapés circulated, the tone of the moaning moderated and became more personal — how the Beijing weather dried out your skin, how the local beer was so thin as to be barely worth drinking, how static made every lift button the source of an electric shock (useful tip: touch the wall, to be grounded, before you touch the button). Gradually, the complaints would be infused with nostalgia — "What I wouldn't give for a decent curry" — before being diluted by general gossip, flirtation and the normal cocktail-party chit-chat.

Ben was still a newbie and knew hardly anyone. He had strategically positioned himself by the end of the drinks table so, by dint of helping people to a glass of something, had struck up one or two conversations. He had also managed to snag a couple of pieces of cheese, a rare and precious item in Beijing. He was now talking to a girl who did something at the British embassy. She had already been in Beijing for a year, so was a good guide to the room, pointing out individuals of note. Most of the attendees seemed to come from other Western embassies. There were the representatives of the big oil companies, now vying for concessions in the Bohai Gulf and South China Sea. The man from Rolls Royce was in attendance with his whole family — nothing to do with the luxury cars, of course, but trying to sell jet engines to the People's Airline. The girl — she was called Angela — was particularly scathing about the representatives of the big international banks: "They've got nothing to do. Just sit around waiting for the day when they might be awarded a licence and start to do some actual business. I see them on the embassy tennis court on a Monday morning."

Somewhere between her second gin-and-tonic and the third spring roll, Angela's commentary moved on to the embassy and the political games that went on there. Her job was essentially clerical "But I get treated like a spy, just like everyone else in the embassy." She seemed happy to talk, perhaps glad of a fresh pair of ears, and Ben gave her his full attention. The man she had replaced had apparently married a local girl.

"It's rather frowned upon, you know. Nobody actually said anything, but you could see it wasn't going to do his career any favors. They're back in London now, but I hear she doesn't like it—the strange food and customs, the rain—and misses her relatives. It must be tough, when you've never even been abroad, suddenly to be transported to completely alien surroundings. At least I had a rough idea of what I was letting myself in for when I accepted this posting. I have the job to keep me busy, colleagues to talk to and I get one flight back home each year. Even if I don't like it, I know it's only going to last two or three years before I'm sent somewhere else. I feel a bit sorry for him—the chap with the local wife. He ought to leave the service and try to get some job back here. Otherwise, I wouldn't be surprised if it ends in divorce. It wouldn't be the first cross-cultural marriage to go astray."

She shook herself, as if fending off unpleasant thoughts. "Anyway, what are you doing this Sunday? There are a bunch of us heading up to the Old Summer Palace. The lake is frozen, so there is going to be some skating. Can you skate?"

"Well, I've only tried once..."

"You'll be fine. The Friendship Hotel is on the way, so we can pick you up. See you then."

She raised her glass and moved off into the crowd. Left alone with his glass of wine and cheese cube on a stick, Ben listened to the conversation behind him—a foreigner updating a friend about his progress with Mandarin lessons.

"Well, I can ask questions now. It's just that I don't understand the answers."

CHAPTER NINE
Outing I

So Ben had, for him, a packed social schedule for the weekend. On Saturday afternoon, after a half-day's work, he took a taxi to the address he had been given for the cinema. It did not look much like one, but a crowd jostled in front of a ticket window, and he did eventually spot a poster for the film *Cold Night*. So he was in the right place, but just a little early and attracting some unwanted attention. He could hear mutterings of *waiguoren* (foreigner). Occasionally there would be a "Hello!" from youths, who would then hurry away, giggling at their own audacity. He decided, as he was early, he might as well buy the tickets so joined the—well, it wasn't really a queue, more a scrum. He waited patiently but, after five minutes, had not made any progress and was still in the scrum's back row.

"Can I help you?"

He turned and looked up. He had been asked this question, in deliberate English, by a tall soldier in full khaki uniform.

"Well, I am just trying to buy two tickets to the 3 o'clock showing, but don't seem to be... "

"If you give me two renminbi, I will buy them for you."

Slightly taken aback, Ben doubtfully unrolled two grubby notes from his purse and handed them over.

"That would be great. Thank you very much."

"You wait here."

"Okay."

Given the soldier's height, it was easy to follow his peaked hat with red star wading through the crowd. Within two minutes he was back. "Here you are," he said, handing over what looked like two bus tickets. "Thank you." Ben hesitated, expecting some follow-up request. But that was it, and the soldier strode away, job well done.

That was when Miss Peng arrived.

"Hi Ben! I see you have already got the tickets. That's good. Let's go in."

The movie was surprisingly entertaining. It was set in the Kuomintang's war-time capital of Chongqing. The villainous Japanese soldier was a stock character on Chinese TV, but here the situation was handled with more subtlety than usual. Pan Hong was excellent in her role as put-upon heroine with divided loyalties, and the camera work was subtle. The movie was, however, only part of the show.

When he first entered, Ben's feet crunched on something. The concrete floor was covered with the husks of sunflower seeds, which were clearly the Chinese audience's equivalent of popcorn. He had already tried sunflower seeds, given their popularity as a snack, but had been underwhelmed — so much effort for so little reward. The process required strong teeth, to crack the seed, and a nimble tongue to extract the kernel before spitting out the husk. When not eating, the audience discussed the merits of the film while it was still showing, which was a little disconcerting. At least Ben could see cuddling going on in the back row, so there was some point of similarity with movie going in the West. As the film approached its climax, a small boy got up from the row behind (there appeared to be no age restrictions), stepped into the aisle, unfurled himself, and started to pee. As the audience seats were on a slight rake, the urine wound its way, Nile-like, towards the front of the stalls, leaving little shoals of seed husks in its wake.

After the show, they collected their bikes, and chatted for a while, as they pushed them side by side along the narrow alleys. They had both enjoyed the movie, but wondered, in real life, whether the heroine would have been so self-sacrificing in her decision to put duty before emotion. He asked her about a series of white posters pasted to walls advertising some event, each with a red tick across them.

"That? Oh, it is an advert for an execution at the Worker's Stadium."

"And the tick?"

"That means it has already been carried out. The parents get charged for the bullet used to execute their child, you know." Ben was about to make a comment about the cruelty of such a procedure but bit his tongue. It had not been so many decades, he supposed, since public hangings in London.

By now it was dark and cold. There seemed to be no warm place for them to continue their talk, no café or welcoming pub. The small local restaurants were strictly utilitarian, with plastic sheets on the tables and fluorescent lighting. So she said goodbye, and he said he would call.

Chapter Ten
Outing II

They picked him up from the Friendship at 10:00 a.m. on Sunday. The vehicle was a smart, imported Toyota Hiace van with diplomatic number plates. It was full—all foreigners. The girl from TGIF, Angela, introduced Ben. He had seen some of them before at the party; new faces included a Finn called Miko and a chap from British Airways wearing a fine wool hat with a bobble. The Toyota was out of the hotel gates and headed north before the introductions were finished.

It was another typical Beijing winter's day, cold but bright, so much preferable to a damp, gray London winter. As they headed away from the city, traffic was sparse. It mostly consisted of battered trucks that must have looked ancient as soon as they came off the production line. The most popular brand of lorry seemed to be Great Leap, a reference to Mao's disastrous economic policy in the early '60s. They overtook a cart pulled by both a gaunt horse and a donkey in harness. The driver, perched on the front of the cart, held a whip. All the vegetation had died back and turned brown. There was no roadside advertising to liven up the scene apart from the occasional red billboard exhorting the onlooker to "Study Dazhai," a model agricultural commune, or "Learn from Lei Feng," a model soldier, who went out of his way to help civilians, and may even have existed. The only other dabs of color were bright orange persimmon fruit, hanging from the leafless trees like Christmas lights. There was little work going on in the fields at this season. The mountains to the North, where the Great Wall snaked across the jagged contours, were flecked with snow.

They stopped before reaching the mountains proper, at the Old Summer Palace, or Yuanmingyuan—Garden of Perfect Brightness. This had been the main palace for the Manchu Qing dynasty until the British and French armies burned it to the ground in 1860. The only structures that remained were ruins of some stone palaces, constructed at the emperor's whim in an exotic in the European Baroque style. The wooden Chinese palaces had all gone up in flames, together with those treasures not 'rescued' by the soldiers. The landscaping, the hills and lakes were still there, giving a clue as to why the Manchu, originally a tribe of nomads from the steppes, might have preferred this palace to the claustrophobic confines of the Forbidden City. A large frozen lake was their destination.

They disgorged from the van. Talk *en route* had been limited, but the crisp, fresh air of the Yuanmingyuan seemed to blow away the Sunday morning fug, and a buzz of anticipation arose. Skates were unpacked from behind the picnic hamper, gloves and woolly hats donned, and the most eager strode down to the lake.

Ben's protestations that he had never skated before were waved off, and he was found a suitable pair of boots. While he was still trying to lace them up, Miko, who had probably been skating since he could walk, sped off across the lake, demonstrating a series of athletic twists and loops. To be fair, he came back as soon as it became clear that Ben's earlier words had not been false modesty. Miko held Ben's arm as he teetered out onto the ice, his feet flopping first left, then right. After fifteen minutes he managed a solo waddle, like a spavined duck, to the amusement of bystanders. As soon as seemed reasonable, he retreated to the bank, acknowledging some ironic applause, and received a thermos of hot soup.

Another group, arriving in a separate van, had brought a surfboard fitted with a sail. Goodness knows where they had acquired it. They took it out onto the lake, but all attempts to make it go were defeated by an almost complete lack of wind. Unable to contribute much to the winter-sport activities, Ben wandered off to look at the palace ruins. Stones, some carved, were scattered over a wide area. Not much was left standing, just the odd portal or wall among the weeds. Clearly, the site had been extensively mined for stone by the locals. There was no apparent attempt at protection or explanation, but the place had a mute, *mutatis mutandis* kind of power.

By the time he wandered back, the picnic was in full swing. There was a good supply of Five Star beer and sandwiches, but it was the hot drinks that saw the greatest demand. Veterans talked of earlier picnics, and other attempts to wrest what pleasure they could from this 'hardship posting': summer lunch amid the old Ming tombs; a champagne breakfast on the Great Wall. Or they talked about what they did on their last R&R trip down to Hong Kong, and what they would do on the next one.

Ben had another chat with Angela, over a thermos of tomato soup. She came from Colchester, about which she was strangely nostalgic. Ben, who had also visited the town, had difficulty reconciling Angela's air-brushed version with the reality. Why hark back to such limited domestic comforts when surrounded by the austere beauty of the Yuanmingyuan?

The subject of business was avoided. It was a Sunday, after all.

les children in other parts of the world, the key challenge
how to ... ... hand - in China, the most
important thing was how to keep them ... A banner of ...
it an ... ... across the ... ...
... which ... ... The ... ... so wildly ...
... had quickly turned out to ... ... color. Pictures on the
... ... as they suddenly appeared in to brightly plastic bags
to grab and later he could unhappily pose, as valuable.
The critical skill was appearing, almost all customers from

Chapter Eleven
Exhibition

He faced a heaving wall of people in blue and khaki. He was manning the company's stand at Equimpex. The show was being held in the Shanghai Exhibition Center, a vast wedding cake of a building that had been a gift from Stalin to the Chinese people at a time when ties with the Soviet Union had been warmer. A couple of the vast halls were temporarily divided into stands for foreign equipment companies and their agents. Oremin's modest stand was decorated with the flyers and posters of the companies it represented. On a bench at one end of the stand stood some liquid chromatography equipment made by a company from Ireland, but pride of place in the middle of the stand was Consarc's mass spectrometer.

In exhibitions in other parts of the world, the key challenge is how to entice visitors on to your stand. In China, the most important thing was how to keep them out. A barrier of tables had been constructed across the front of the stand with only a small entrance, which could, like Thermopylae, be easily defended. Ben had quickly learned not to spread color brochures on the front table as they quickly disappeared into bulging plastic bags to be utilized later, he could only guess, as wallpaper.

The crucial skill was separating potential customers from

timewasters. Appearance was not always a good guide, though the guys wearing Kim Il-sung badges could safely be ignored. North Koreans aside, were they asking the right questions? What was the specific application for which they wanted the equipment, and did that make sense? What organization were they affiliated with? Did they have a foreign-exchange allocation or any likelihood of getting one? Only once these criteria were satisfied would attendees be allowed through the pass to the inner sanctum, to have a closer look at the equipment, to sit at a metal table and chairs for the exchange of name cards and a more detailed discussion with the principals.

It was challenging work. It was not just the technical vocabulary required — there was frequent recourse to hand signals or the drawing of diagrams — but also withstanding the intense blast of tobacco-with-garlic breath blown in the exhibitors' direction. Every thirty minutes or so, Ben would take a quick fresh-air break. With principals and customers in town for the exhibition, the evenings were no less fraught, given the need for corporate entertainment. This exhibition was due to last for three days.

The Shanghai No.5 Special Chemical Works delegation turned up on the afternoon of the first day. They were accompanied by CMIEC Deputy Section Chief Lin and Miss Peng. Ben gave a sign to Vowles and Gordon, who had been lounging at the metal table. They sprang up to welcome the delegation. And so the negotiation began.

The Consarc team knew that the Chemical Works was seriously interested in buying the spectrometer and, as evidenced by CMIEC's involvement, had the foreign currency to buy it. But the Chemical Works team knew that the company did not want to pay for shipping the exhibited equipment all the way back to the UK. Also it would be a feather in the cap for Consarc's executives, having travelled far and at such expense, to make the sale.

The potential customer was a prestigious factory, where the spectrometer's installation could act as an advert to other Chinese companies in the industry; the lure of multiple sales was dangled in front of the foreigners' eyes. Achieving an impressive discount to the list price was most important—CMIEC was keen to prove its usefulness to its 'customer', the Special Chemical Works. Surely installation and training would also be thrown in? And how long would the seller guarantee the equipment? Surely longer than one year! And what about the price of consumables?

And so the negotiations were drawn out over another two meetings, interspersed by further torture-by-baijiu-and-sea slug, for which Vowles was ill prepared, his stomach once more rebelling. *Shui tu bu fu*—"The water and soil does not agree with you"—murmured Mr Lin sympathetically. Eventually the deal was concluded late on the Saturday afternoon, just before the exhibition was to close. Contracts were prepared and signed, hands shaken. Vowles looked grim signing the contract, but once the delegation had gone, he smiled, winked at Ben and mock whispered, "I put up the price before I discounted it."

That evening they celebrated in the bar at the Peace Hotel, where an ancient jazz band provided about the only nightlife available in Shanghai, sadly fallen from its pre-Liberation reputation as "The Paris of the Orient". Fuelled by nothing more than hot tea from thermos bottles set by each music stand, the band did their best with jazz standards. As Ben was to come to learn, they always played the same songs in the same order, to the extent that you could tell the time by them. "The Girl from Ipanema. Must be 8:00 p.m. already." There were some compensations. On this particular evening, a Japanese businessman who had clearly been upcountry for a long time, and had imbibed liberally of the Moutai cocktails on offer, felt called by the band's Carmen medley. He took to the dance floor and, gripping a plastic flower from his table between his teeth, trailed his suit-jacket behind him, matador-style. He was given much encouragement from the audience and finished to a rousing ovation.

The Consarc group wisely restrained themselves to toasting their success with bottles of the weak local beer, ahead of the morrow's long flight home.

CHAPTER TWELVE
Boat Trip

Ben saw her from some distance away, weaving towards him through the Sunday crowds milling by the riverbank. She spotted him and gave a little wave. He realized he must stand out from the crowd—a foreigner in a smart business coat and leather gloves. While waiting, he had already been offered two opportunities to change money, to swap his crisp, clean foreign exchange certificates at the black-market rate for the grubby, less useful renminbi. Once he was approached for English practice. He had found that claiming he was from Romania was the safest and most effective answer to avoid further interaction.

At the exhibition, in between sessions, Miss Peng had tried to teach him some Shanghai dialect. She had been to college in Shanghai and offered to show him around on the Sunday before they both headed back to Peking. A boat trip down the Huangpu had been decided upon, so he was waiting on the Bund by its array of fine art deco skyscrapers, built earlier in the century when Shanghai was still a treaty port. It reminded him of Liverpool; the Mersey and the Huangpu were also a little alike in being the colour of mud.

She bought two tickets at the counter—foreigners had to pay double the local price, presumably in accord with Marx's dictum about "From each according to his ability..." They climbed aboard, up a slippery ramp. The boat resembled a ferry, though its only purpose was tourism, to take visitors down to where the Huangpu emptied into the Yangtse Delta. The propellers churned the opaque yellow water, a sailor expertly cast off and they were away. They stood by the ship's railing, facing west to the city. Xiao Peng explained the old and new names of some of the more prominent buildings. The old names were more romantic but fatally tainted with colonialism: Sassoon's Cathay Hotel had become the Peace Hotel; Broadway Mansions on Suzhou Creek, in its day the largest brick building in the world, had become just the Shanghai Daxia (Shanghai Building); the Astor House Hotel, with its Rainbow Ball room and sepia photographs of Charlie Chaplin and other famous visitors, was now prosaically the Pujiang Hotel.

Miss Peng leaned over the ship railings, a fresh breeze lifting her fringe. "I went to college over there" she said, looking north into Hongkou, "Fudan University".

"What's over there?" Ben said, pointing to the opposite bank.

"That's just Pudong. There's not much to see there." Indeed, the rag-tag collection of warehouses, industrial facilities and low-rise housing compared poorly with the fine display of the Bund on the other side of the river.

There was not much to see as they chugged downriver with the tide. "Seagull" was a popular brand name in Shanghai but there was a notable lack of any wildlife. The land was absolutely flat. The Bund aside, Shanghai presented its working face to the river, just like railways do in those minutes before one pulls into a city center. More interesting were the other boats on the river, from huge ore carriers, down to small tugs, carrying a family and a few sacks of cement, and flying a flag of drying laundry. The ship names were Marxist or patriotic. A coal barge called

Struggle 23 chugged past. Ben even spotted a small submarine, part of the People's Navy. Without thinking, he raised his small camera to take a photo, but Xiao Peng pressed it down. "Don't do that." She looked to both sides to see if anyone had noticed.

They had a nice, if careful, chat as they drifted along, about the exhibition, about travel plans for the next few weeks, about their families.

"Are you a Communist Party member?" he asked.

"No. Why would you think so?"

"I thought you had to be if you wanted to work for a government organization."

"No, not necessarily."

"Wouldn't it help, with promotion and the like?"

"I suppose so. It just never happened. I always planned to go abroad to study or work."

"But surely being a party member would help with that, too?"

"Only if you go under government sponsorship, which carries various obligations. You can also get private sponsorship, if you have a relative overseas, able to pay."

"I see," Ben said.

Fortunately, at that moment, the big reveal of the Yangtse opened before them, so wide that the other side could not be seen. This gave them another topic for a while. The ferry swung around and headed back upriver, its engine working harder against the ebbing tide.

"Would you like to come over to my house next week?" Miss Peng asked, tentatively.

"But won't that get you in trouble. You know, with me being a counter-revolutionary and all?"

"No, it's Okay just for tea. My parents will be there. And my sister, probably."

"Well, that would be nice. I don't have any travel coming up for the next two weeks. Just let me know what evening suits."

"Thursday?" "Sure."

They were then silent for a while, watching the industrial scene drift by. A steel works. A power station surrounded by mountains of coal. Miss Peng's next question appeared a complete non-sequitur. "Does your company supply cobalt cathodes?"

"It's possible. I have not been working there too long, but it's quite possible. I can check when I get back into the office tomorrow. Why do you ask?"

"I was talking to a factory that has demand."

"What size should I ask them to offer, if they have supply?"

"Fifteen tonnes. CIF Hong Kong."

"OK. I'll check." Ben said, nonchalantly. The submarine had gone by the time they reached that stretch of the river.

CHAPTER THIRTEEN
Diary

4/4/83

I returned from Shanghai last night. The plane was delayed, as usual, so I did not get home till late. Yesterday I spent the day with Ben. I asked him to meet my father. I am not sure whether it is the right thing to do. I think they will get on OK, but it may be too soon. Perhaps I will find an excuse to postpone it. The exhibition went well. Old Zhang even thanked me for my help! He must be getting soft in his old age.

7/4/83

There was a terrible sandstorm today. Going to work, I had to get off and push my bike. At least I have my excuse to cancel tea. Maybe I'll postpone it for a week or so. I passed on the cobalt price to my father.

CHINA DAILY

Thursday, April 7, 1983   2, Jintai Xilu, Beijing   Price: 10 fen; 15 fen (airmail)

Blowin' in the wind

A gale roared in from the northwest yesterday to batter Beijing for almost five hours. The sky turned yellow with dust; girls wrapped their heads in gauze kerchiefs; and most cyclists had to dismount and push their bikes.

China Daily/Xinhua

CHAPTER FOURTEEN
The Hash

Back in the office in Beijing, Ben had added the cobalt cathode inquiry to Monday evening's telex. The answer came "Will revert. Pls advise what client?" Ben did not want to call Miss Peng again in front of his colleagues. On the last occasion, Shirley had given him a funny look. So he waited until they were both out visiting a client.

"Prosperity Pencil," Miss Peng said.

"A pencil maker? But why would a pencil maker want cobalt? I thought it was used in special steel alloys, for aviation applications and..."

"It is complicated. I can explain when we meet."

"Okay."

So his telex that evening read: "Prosperity Pencils, Hong Kong. I know. Will revert details next week, but pls indicate price if poss."

The offer came in on Thursday: $24.75/lb CIF Hong Kong. He rang Peng to tell her, making clear, as instructed, that it was an indicative offer only, and she should let him know if she needed it firming up. She cancelled the visit to her home. Ben was both disappointed and relieved.

That weekend's entertainment was the Hash, or a meeting of

the Hash House Harriers to give it the full name. This involved cross-country running and beer drinking, neither of which was Ben's forte, but it was a chance to widen his social circle, and he got to see bits of Beijing he would not otherwise know about.

The storm had blown itself out and Saturday was a fine Beijing spring afternoon, still cold, but sunny. A sizeable crowd had gathered, mostly foreigners. Ben's favorite t-shirt, which gave some flavor of this cosmopolitan crowd, read "Khartoum Marathon 1981". The clever part about this venerable expat institution, perhaps the only clever part, was that a track had been laid ahead of time by the 'hares', with several false tracks that would handicap the stronger runners. In this way, the participants, who ranged in ability from evening strollers to iron men, could finish at roughly the same time. Today's run, Ben was pleased to see, was to be through a relatively flat agricultural area north of Beijing. It was the start of the planting season, so farmers were out in the fields, tending to their vegetable patches. Goodness knows what they made of the long line of foreigners jogging past in colorful shorts and fancy trainers.

Ben was getting the hang of it. He watched the fastest runners chase up false trails and have to double back. By the time he reached a chalk sign marking two possible routes, the correct one was usually obvious. "Well, this isn't so bad" he thought, becoming a little cocky as, despite his earlier fears, he was perhaps in the middle of the pack. He was tiring, but dusk was starting to fall, so there could not be too much further to go. He caught sight of the leaders in the distance over to his right. The path wanted him to go left, but he had the brainwave that he could take a short cut through the cabbage patch to the right, cutting off a huge corner. Running through cabbages was not easy, especially as the light was now fading fast, but up ahead he saw a level patch. If he put on a spurt of speed here, he could actually finish well up the order. He took a leap onto the level patch of ground to discover, unfortunately, that it was a cesspit. With a desperate lunge, he just managed to grab the side before he was fully immersed. He dragged himself out and, covered in shit from shoulders to shoes, jogged forlornly towards the finish. One farmer, taking pity, showed him to a standpipe so he could clean himself up. It was cold, but there was really no alternative. He did not 'knock on' to the subsequent beer-drinking session, but cycled damply home. The only silver lining, as he discovered later, was that he never again suffered from 'Beijing belly'. The dip in the cesspit seemed to have given him a one-shot immunization against food poisoning.

CHAPTER FIFTEEN
Tea

"Who are you visiting?" the security guard asked in a tone both bored and hostile, adjusting a beribboned cap that made him look like a colonel in the Ruritanian army. Ben gave him the name and address.

"Wait here. I will call up to check." Seeing Ben looking at his uniform, the guard straightened an epaulette.

The postponed tea had been fixed for a Sunday afternoon. The Peng family lived in an insalubrious, low-rise cement block. Someone had started cooking. These pleasanter dinner smells were layered over an ambient base note of fermenting vegetables, carbon monoxide and urine. There had been a rain shower earlier in the week, the first rain Ben had seen in Beijing since his arrival. A spindly poplar in the corner of the compound had responded with a green fuzz of buds.

"Ok. You can go up. Doorway on the left. Third floor." Ben squeezed past the bicycles at the bottom of the cement stairs, clutching his gift, a tin of imported shortbread biscuits, which he had bought at the Friendship Store using his foreign exchange certificates. He climbed the dimly lit stairs and only had to tap once on the door before it was pulled open. Miss Peng was waiting there.

"Come in, come in. Did you find the place Okay? Are you all right?"

"Yes, fine. Should I take off my shoes?" he said, taking off his shoes, grateful that he was wearing socks without a hole. He was, he realized, rather nervous. He had been in China some months, but this was the first time he had been invited into a Chinese person's home.

"Come in, come through. My father is in here." Xiao Peng was clearly also nervous. "This is my father. Father, this is Ben."

"It is a pleasure to meet you, Mr Peng." He was a stocky man in a grey jacket, balding and wearing round reading spectacles. An open book was face-down on the table. He hurriedly removed the glasses. He had a mole on his chin from which a long hair had been allowed to grow.

"And I am pleased to meet you, Ben. I have heard a lot about you."

"All good, I hope?"

"Oh, yes. Pretty good." Mr Peng smiled. "Please sit down here. Let's have some tea. I will get some hot water."

As Mr Peng was turning, Ben remembered the tin box he was clutching.

"I brought this small gift for your wife."

"Thank you." Peng turned into a galley kitchen that led off the living room. Xiao Peng smiled encouragingly. The room was plainly decorated and simply furnished. Apart from the table and stools, there was a writing desk and glass-fronted cupboard filled with books and mounted photographs. In one, Ben recognized a younger Peng in uniform, with a group of colleagues. The only decoration on the walls was a calendar by the desk and a hanging scroll of calligraphy, the meaning of which he could not make out. The room was no better lit than the stairwell. On the table, which was protected by a thick plastic sheet, was an impressive

Chinese tea set. The father was obviously keen on tea.

"What type of tea do you prefer?" Mr Peng asked, returning.

"I like Tie Guanyin. But really any Longjing or green tea would be fine. I am not so keen on Pu'er. I find it rather bitter," said Ben, belatedly hoping that the father was not a Pu'er aficionado.

"Well, I think you will like this one. Lung Jing. Fresh from Zhejiang." Mr Peng then set about the complex procedure of making tea as it should be done — pot warming, emptying and steeping. The result was a tiny thimbleful of tea each. Ben lifted his cup, carefully smelt the aroma then sipped, followed by an appreciative sigh.

"Do you like the taste?"

"Yes. The flavor is excellent."

It was. He didn't need to pretend. "Where do you get your tea?"

Mr Peng gave a full explanation of the tea merchant he had used for years, conveniently sited near his office. That led on to a discussion of his work in ship design. Ben started to inquire further as to what aspect of ships he was involved with, but dropped the subject quickly as soon as he gathered that they were discussing ships for the Navy. Mr Peng sounded as though he was someone senior in the ministry. The teacups were re-filled. Ben was questioned in turn and gave a sanitized and potted account of his short life to date.

"Would you like to try some dried persimmons with your tea?" The father gestured with his chin at Xiao Peng, who went into the galley to find them.

"I understand you met my daughter through her work unit?" he said more quietly.

"Yes, she has been so kind. Showing me round Beijing. And also Shanghai, of course."

"Shanghai?"

"Yes, we both were working at the Equipment Expo there. Having attended college there, she…"

"Ah, I see."

Xiao Peng returned with a plate of dried persimmons, which were chewy and sweet, complementing the tartness of the tea.

"Do you play Xiangqi?"

"Sorry?"

"Chinese chess" chimed in Xiao Peng. "My father organizes a league at his office."

"Well, I like Western chess and have played Chinese chess a couple of times, but…"

"Let's have a game." The tea set was pushed to one side and a Xiangqi set fetched from a drawer in the bureau.

"Are your wife and younger daughter not here today?"

"They had to go out. Will you go first?"

The game did not last long. Ben was thrashed.

"How about a return match?"

"Well, I think I ought to…" but Mr Peng was already repositioning the pieces. This game lasted a little longer, but still resulted in another resounding defeat.

"It seems as though I need some practice," Ben said, pulling a face.

"Keep at it. I see promise." Mr Peng smiled.

"Well, I'm not sure. I better be going but thank you for the delicious tea. And the persimmons were particularly good."

"Take some with you. Here, wrap a couple in this tissue." As Ben stood up, he carefully inserted the persimmons into his coat pocket; he would later, inadvertently, sit on them.

"Thank you for coming. I am pleased that my daughter has been able to show you around Beijing a bit."

In a parting shake of hands, Mr Peng held his hand slightly longer than strictly necessary while giving him an appraising look. The kind of look you might gi_____ey when asked to guess its weight. As Ben turned to go, h___said "I believe my daughter talked to about the cobalt?"

"Yes, she did mention it, and I was just going to…"

"It will be good if we can work something out. It is for a contact. It will be to our… mutual benefit. And there be further commodities which we require."

He gestured to Xiao Peng. "My daughter will show you out."

He held up a hand in valediction.

Ben and Xiao Peng clumped down the stairs, whispering.

"I hope that was Okay?" he said.

"He likes you. I could tell when he brought out the persimmons."

"Ah, yes."

Ben patted his pocket.

"And it was good how you let him win at Xiangqi so convincingly."

It was dark in the stairwell, but Ben could make out the ironic smile.

"You could have given me some warning. And what was that about the cobalt?"

Xiao Peng's face turned serious. She hesitated, then seemed to decide something.

"You must not say anything, but Prosperity Pencil is owned by a relative. The end-user is a contact of my father at Norinco. If we route the cobalt through Hong Kong, then there will be a margin. There will be some money offshore to pay for overseas study should I or my sister… "

"Oh, I see."

Ben thought for a minute. "I don't see that should affect me. If the price is acceptable and the cash to pay for it is there then…"

"Thank you." She took his hand and leaned forward. He gave

her hand a squeeze. _ll _ _ _ morrow."

As they left the shadow of the stairwell, she let go of his hand. She waved farewell at a distance when they reached the guardhouse. The guard followed his exit with his eyes. Scowling. Ben gave him a salute.

At the office next morning, Ben asked about Norinco. It was the state-owned corporation in charge of the arms business.

CHAPTER SIXTEEN
Diary

17/4/83

Father met Ben today. It would probably have been better if I'd arranged for my mother to be there as well. More welcoming. Father was brusque. He does not have much experience dealing with foreigners. I know he is only trying to protect his daughter, but still... <u>two</u> games of Xiangqi was a bit cruel. Ben did his best. I hope we have not frightened him off.

Chapter Seventeen
Disco

Dictators seem to have a deep suspicion of pop music. Folk songs or some suitably updated Peking Opera are fine, but modern music is a step too far. In this Cromwellian prejudice, the communists were joined by the nationalists, as Ben remembered from clandestine dance parties held during his summer language study in Taiwan. In Beijing, there were discos in two or three hotels designed for foreigners only. Ostensibly a passport was needed to get in, but Ben's inquiries had revealed that, with a sufficiently forthright approach, a foreigner could smuggle in a local.

Xiao Peng had let it be known that she wanted to sample the bright lights. The best of the limited selection of discos was, apparently, held at the Minzu Hotel on a Friday night, so preparations were made. They met in the lobby of the hotel at 7:00 p.m., which seemed to Ben terribly early for that sort of thing, but when in Rome... He saw Xiao Peng had made an effort to locate an outfit suitable for the mission. For the first time since they'd met, she had applied some lipstick and a little eye shadow. Ben, straight from the office, had made no such effort, but trusted in the essential strangeness of foreigners to see him through. They decided that nourishment was required before assaulting the dance floor, so they demolished two bowls of jia-jiang noodles in the hotel restaurant. Suitably fortified, they headed upstairs.

They could hear the music as they walked down the corridor. Boney M—a classic. Swirling colored lights beckoned from the dim room beyond, but first a check-point had to be negotiated. A trestle table had been drawn up alongside the door and at it lounged two dudes in ill-fitting suits. Ben strode up confidently and demanded "Two tickets for the dancing". He didn't know what the Chinese word for disco was, or even if there was one.

Dude One looked at Ben. He then gave Xiao Peng the full up-and-down, from pumps to artfully coiffed hair, and was starting to curl his lip when Ben said "She's with me."

"That will be fifty yuan."

A bit steep, but then... Ben started to uncurl some RMB notes from his purse. "Foreign exchange certificates only," Dude Two said disdainfully. Ben replaced the grubby RMB notes in his purse, replacing them reluctantly with crisp, clean FEC, which were worth about three times more at black-market rates.

"A drink is included" conceded Dude One, reluctantly. Ben nodded, took his tickets, and they entered. Despite the early hour, it was busy. There were couples and groups, both on the dance floor (the music had changed to Olivia Newton John) and at tables around the room's edges. In the dark, it was difficult to assess the portion of foreigners and locals because of the presence of overseas Chinese. One notable sub-group consisted of black Africans. Many students were brought over on scholarships from politically sympathetic African countries. They were then, rather cruelly it seemed to Ben, assigned to colleges in the coldest parts of China. He had always felt a little sorry for them, as they stood shivering, disdained by the locals. Here, however, they were in their element.

Xiao Peng led the way to a table and hailed a waiter. The drinks included in the ticket price turned out all to be soft, so of no help in loosening inhibitions about making a fool of himself on the dance floor. They settled for some of the ubiquitous orange Fanta, and his tickets were collected. "Shall we?" said Ben, indicating the dance floor.

As the loud music made conversation untenable, they spent most of their two hours dancing. Ben tried out his moves, mostly derived from Saturday Night Fever and a long acquaintance with Top of the Pops. He tried not to think what he must look like, and eventually succeeded. Xiao Peng said that this was her first disco, but she had clearly been practicing in front of a mirror. She made up in enthusiasm for what she perhaps lacked in finesse, but who was he to talk? There was much smiling, and perspiration flowed freely. In terms of the music, the highlight was definitely "YMCA" with the crowd triumphantly throwing themselves into the letter shapes required by the lyrics.

In one of the Fanta breaks, Ben sat catching his breath, admiring the dancing of the Africans. He was not the only admirer; the Africans had attracted a posse of Chinese girls, for whom they were providing an impromptu disco teach-in. On a long table at the back, a group of Chinese youths seemed less impressed. There was muttering among the abandoned boyfriends and some angry looks.

"Do you think we should be going?" said Ben, indicating the back of the room with a nod of his head.

"Okay," she said, reluctantly. As they made their way towards the exit, he asked, "What do you think?"

"Not bad" she said, and blew out her cheeks, fanning herself in an effort to cool down. Ben gave Dudes One and Two a cheery wave as they left: "Nice orange juice."

either the old Shanghai cabs or the new generation of VW Santanas, based on an outmoded Italian model. The best to best spell for was a scarred large limousine, like a Crown or a Red Flag limousine, though the I-car windows used to induce undying curios

There was little else to drive. Bicycles were mostly ...tically for ...buses or ...

Chapter Eighteen
Soft Class

Travelling around China was not easy. For Ben, it was not a question of travel restrictions—unlike diplomats or reporters, businessmen could travel most places, apart from Tibet, which required special permission. It was just the lack of infrastructure and systems. Driving was a very slow way to travel far. Most roads were two lanes at best and infested with walking tractors and donkey carts. It was worse at night when truck drivers would save electricity by driving without lights until within ten meters of an oncoming car, when they would flash them at full beam. In the autumn, farmers would spread grain over the road to dry. (Ben had wondered why some of his rice tasted rather rubbery...) The cars themselves were not terribly comfortable— either the old Shanghai autos or the new generation of VW Santanas, based on an outmoded Brazilian model. The best to be hoped for was a second-hand imported Toyota Crown or a Red Flag limousine, though the latter were reserved for higher-ranking cadres.

Flying was little easier. Delays were endemic, especially for afternoon flights. The fleet boasted many old Russian Antonovs and Tupolevs—the latter sported a fourth wheel under the tail to stop them from falling over. The pride of the fleet was a consignment of Tridents bought second-hand from Pakistan Airlines. A bigger problem than the dated hardware, however, was the software: it was impossible to book a return flight. The first task upon arrival in a new city, therefore, was finding a way to leave it. This was exasperating when trying to plan complicated itineraries for visiting delegations.

A slow but reliable train was often the default option. So it was that Ben found himself boarding a train at Beijing West railway station, with an American and a Japanese businessman both from a furnace-maker, for a thirty-six-hour journey to a cemented-carbide manufacturer in Hunan. They were in 'soft class'. As a communist society, China did not have first- and second-class seating, you understand. Similarly, for air travel you could pay a premium to travel in *Tou deng* (literally 'head class') seats at the front of the plane. This actually made very little difference — perhaps an extra hard-boiled egg in the lunch box.

For travel on a train, however, the differences between 'soft class' and 'hard class' were substantial. This was firstly a matter of numbers — there were four berths in a soft-class compartment whereas in hard class the only limit seemed to be however many would fit. The berths in soft class were also relatively comfortable, at least compared with the wooden planks in hard class. And soft-class berths carried assigned seat numbers, so there wasn't the mad scramble for places seen in hard class. Last but not least, soft class came with a hot-water thermos, regularly refilled by a tea lady, with little paper bags of tea leaves and mugs on lace doilies.

Departure was uneventful — soft-class tickets brought with them a superior waiting room and separate platform gate. Once tickets had been clipped and the view out of the darkening window had lost its charm, Ben's delegation busied itself with items brought along to help pass the dreary journey. For the Japanese, this was a tiny new personal computer, which he was figuring out how to use. For the American, it was a bottle of Jack Daniels bought in duty-free. For Ben, it was the Raj Quartet. Train travel in China was well suited to the consumption of multi-volume sagas. In his role as native guide, Ben had already suggested to his clients that they lay off the railway food, which anyway wasn't good, if they were to avoid unnecessary visits to the toilet. Public toilets in China were always best avoided, but trying to balance over the hole against the jogging of the train made the procedure particularly hazardous in this case. Ben confined himself to tea, an apple and a type of peanut-flavoured cracker from Xiamen he had discovered. He also accepted a glass of whisky later as an aid to sleep. Sleep was not easy, despite the whisky, as the train made several night stops, at one of which—he did not recognize the name—there was a change of engine, which entailed much shunting and clanking of buffers. In between these disturbances, the American snored and, once he put his computer down, the Japanese ground his teeth. You got to know your clients well, rather too well, on these long China trips.

Next morning, once Ben wearied of the goings on of the British Raj, he plugged in his Sony Walkman and daydreamed while watching China trundle by. As summer was advancing the fields were busy with farmers, singly or in groups, spraying or hoeing. Fruit trees and vegetable plots gave way to more rice paddies as they headed south. He kept a mental track of progress, matching the names of stations to his memory of the map on the wall in his office. It was odd how similar most Chinese cities looked. Perhaps it was because they were mostly built on a flat plain, so there was little to distinguish them in terms of topography. The effect of China's recent turbulent history meant that surprisingly few antiquities survived. Most cities appeared to have been hastily constructed from the same concrete, bricks and bathroom tiles, with no budget for architectural flourishes.

Ben composed a letter to his parents. He thought about Xiao Peng, whose name would not appear in the letter, of course. He thought of the way she fanned herself to cool down at the disco. The cobalt deal had gone through with remarkable ease. He had mentioned the Norinco angle to London, but that did not seem to be an issue, and his boss had been very happy with the margin on the deal. The pencil company had opened a letter of credit, so all was well that ends well. Xiao Peng had mentioned something about helping organize a trip overseas, but it had not been convenient to go into detail over the phone.

Eventually, saddle-sore, they rolled into Zhuzhou, a dour industrial city in Hunan that was China's production base for cemented carbide (a hard material used in cutting tools, such as drill bits). They were met at the station by a driver from the company, and the normal round of events commenced: factory tour, technical discussion, negotiation and banquet. Frog seemed to be the local speciality, and there was an unappetizing stew made of *Wawa yu*. When Ben sought to identify this, he was told it was a fish that had legs and cried like a baby. When he looked it up later in the dictionary, it turned out, unfortunately, to be a rare giant salamander. The local cadres were a hard-drinking bunch, but the American, well-practiced as evidenced by his dispatch of the bourbon on the train, held up his end well. It was counted a moral victory when the factory head, rising to make a valedictory speech, put his hand in the soup and had to be helped away from the table. They had earlier established that their furnace appeared suitable to the needs of the factory, which had an allocation of foreign exchange. China Non-ferrous Import-Export Corp in Beijing would be handling the import, so all seemed set fair. Best of all, Ben managed to snag three tickets for a plane back to Beijing.

CHAPTER NINETEEN
The Barter Trade

The trips that Ben enjoyed most were to China's northwestern provinces. These distant provinces, such as Gansu, Qinghai and Xinjiang, were amongst the poorest parts of China, and traveling there was difficult, so Yu and Shirley were happy to leave these trips to Ben. But the area was rich in minerals, and the local trade bureaus, being less visited, were generally friendlier, so there was business to be done. The rugged terrain and sense of distance from home brought out the hidden Lawrence of Arabia that lurks in many a young Englishman with a strong imagination. The deserts, the mountains, the big sky gave more scope for Ben to think himself back to the days of the Silk Road. There were fewer pylons and factories, fewer modern intrusions, to have to mask out.

Whenever Ben visited a new place, he tried to find time to walk around it. Sometimes the only time available was just before or after meetings, but occasionally trips could be extended into a weekend or public holiday. Watching though a car window was no substitute for allowing his own dusty shoes to pace out a town's alleys and backstreets. In the far west, this was particularly rewarding. A dental surgery open to the street attracted a lively audience. At a butcher's stand, a goat's head hung on a hook, reminding him of the Chinese saying "To hang out a sheep's head and sell dog meat". There were plenty of unpleasant smells, especially in the summer heat, but there were pleasant ones too. Ben enjoyed loitering in markets by shops selling spices. A Uyghur tradesman took time to explain his wares to this rare foreign visitor. Ben won a few smiles by dropping the few words of Uyghur he had learned into the conversation: "kop rahmat" (thanks), "khayr khosh" (goodbye).

China's shortage of foreign currency often caused a reversion to an earlier form of trade: barter. This is what had led to the horrible Hungarian buses that now polluted the streets of Shanghai. They were far from the best buses the world had to offer, but Hungary had, apparently, been willing to accept Chinese chickens in payment. In the far west of China, the shortage of foreign exchange was even more severe. This led to Ben's best deal yet, setting aside the cobalt trade, which had fallen into his lap, so to speak.

The dusty town of Lanzhou, capital of Gansu Province, hung under a permanent yellowish cloud created by a petrochemical factory upwind from the city center. On the north bank of the river a white stupa, built by the Mongols in memory of a fallen Tibetan king, pierced the gloom. During the Long March, 10,000 men died here capturing a strategic bridge from a Muslim warlord. The main thing Lanzhou now had to offer was tasty hand-pulled noodles, and, because of the big local Muslim population, some good lamb dishes. Later, Lanzhou was to be home to another Englishman, the footballer Paul Gascoigne, who played briefly for the local football team. Lanzhou proved not to be a good location for a recovering alcoholic.

In 1983, the local Minmetal branch listed among its products for export silicon metal. This was not the high-spec version used in semiconductors, but a more primitive rock-like material with various industrial applications, including as an additive in the refining of aluminium. Now Oremin had the agency for an Australian aluminium producer to export to China, so the opportunity for a deal was apparent. Ben dutifully reported back Gansu's silicon specifications and price indication on his evening telex and received a positive reply. A contract was drawn up to swap a specific amount of aluminium ingots for a given amount of silicon. A celebratory dinner was organized, in which sea slugs were mercifully absent; there can be few cities which are further from the sea than Lanzhou.

On a walk next morning, whiling away the time before heading to the airport, Ben saw another side of the city. Somewhere in the dusty outskirts he heard the wailing of sirens. The noise was louder than could be generated by just one or two police cars or ambulances. This was a whole convoy, and it was coming in his direction. He ducked into a doorway. There were locals walking away, heads down, some clutching pink slips of paper. An army truck came round the corner. There was a man standing behind a machine gun mounted on the cab roof. This was followed by a bus with bars across the windows. Men with shaved heads looked out at him from behind the bars. Then came another armed truck and another bus. The procession slowly wended its way out of town, still wailing. When it had gone, Ben picked up a discarded pink sheet. It was headed "Anti-crime campaign".

The silicon/aluminium barter deal, after initial logistical difficulties, proved successful. On the first shipment the customer reported that there was a problem with sizing—some of the individual lumps of silicon metal were too large. In the next shipment, the sizing was a correct, but a hammer was discovered in the cargo. Ben had the sorry vision of shaven-headed men in a quarry hammering away at rocks under the hot Gansu sun.

敦煌賓館

DUNHUANG GUEST HOUSE

Arrived last night at 1 o'clock after a hair-
raising 2 hour ride across the desert. There was
just us, a skyful of the brightest stars I've seen,
an unspring 1950 shanghai car, and a road that
~~would~~ makes the Cresta Run look like a bowling
alley. After 2 hours I felt as if I'd entered a
particularly gruelling rodeo.

We saw the Mogao caves today. It is a
cliffside in the desert pock-marked with natural

Shirley's due date drew near, and she and Yu headed back to Hong Kong to have the baby. It was now high summer, typically a quiet time in the Beijing office, and Ben was adjudged able to hold down the fort in Shirley and Yu's absence. After some initial nervousness, Ben settled into the daily schedule of an office where the decibel level was now distinctly lower.

It was scorching hot, but at least Beijing's heat was dry. The hotel's air-conditioning struggled, drowning out the loud whirring of the cicadas. In the evenings families sat outside their houses. Occasionally a group gathered around a TV, the power line of which snaked back into a plug inside. Ben cycled past one enterprising chap reading by the changing illumination of a traffic light. There was a government regulation that work could officially be suspended if the temperature reached 37 degrees C, but, mysteriously, it always seemed to peak at 36. Ben saw more of Xiao Peng, cycling with her to visit some of Beijing's many historic sites. Occasionally, he joined picnics organized by the TGIF crowd, though activities were much reduced as many expats headed back to their own countries for summer holidays.

In one strange interlude, Ben was called upon to pretend to be Irish. Ireland's trade minister, and head of the Labour

Party, a certain Mr Cluskie, was paying an official visit to boost Irish exports to China. In his role promoting chromatography equipment from Shannon, Ben had had dealings with the Irish embassy, and found them helpful. They were a lot more helpful than the British embassy, where trade was clearly a poor cousin to intelligence; the Irish diplomats privately referred to their British equivalents as "the cocktail party boys". So Ben was happy to pretend to be Irish. It meant he got to accompany the delegation to a meeting with China's trade minister, Wu Yi, one of the few women ever to hold a seat in the Politburo. The reception was slick, and Minister Wu charming; it was interesting to see the face the Chinese Communist Party presented to visiting politicians. Wu was well briefed and referred to Cluskie's background as a butcher in complimentary terms. Ben was able to make a contribution as one of the few Chinese-speaking Irish.

The peaceful summer life faded as September arrived sparking a revival in visiting clients. Late September brought a peak in delegations. All Beijing's hotels were full. There was already a scanning electron microscope salesman sleeping on the office couch. An engineer from an American crystal-puller company was expected that evening and had nowhere booked. Ben was becoming desperate as he hit the phone, trying to ask a favor from friends and acquaintances, but everyone was in the same fix. That's when Ben had a brainwave and made his first big mistake.

Shirley and Yu were still down in Hong Kong, Shirley having just given birth to a bouncing baby boy, so their apartment in the Friendship Hotel stood empty. He could temporarily put the engineer there. The engineer would only be in town for a couple of days, before heading upcountry. Ben knew the concierge, so it took relatively little work to persuade the guards to open the flat for a foreigner who would be arriving that night. In retrospect,

Ben should perhaps have cleared the matter with Shirley, but he was in a hurry and sure that, in the circumstances, the couple would not mind. They did. Ben received the following chilling fax from Hong Kong:

"We take your action very seriously. Get Fisher out or we will have the hotel remove him forcibly. Confirm immediately."

The idea of some stranger having slept in their bed seemed to incense Yu and Shirley. It should not have mattered, but the engineer was black, and this somehow seemed to make everything a lot worse. Ben's relationship with the couple never really recovered.

Chapter Twenty-One
Another Mistake

The trading firm for which Ben worked could be characterized as buccaneering. The founder had been on Britain's first 'ice-breaker' mission to the People's Republic and continued doing business there throughout the chaos of the Cultural Revolution. Old hands told stories of how all negotiations at the Canton Trade Fair had been preceded by a reading of Mao's Little Red Book. So it was a company that took risks and reached parts where other companies would fear to tread. One reflection of this maverick spirit was that the partners from the various global offices would all meet once a year for an adventure in some exotic location. This year it had been decided that the partners and wives would hold a camel race in the Gobi Desert. Ben, having already shown his interest in China's far west, was tasked with organizing it.

Traveling around China as an individual was difficult enough. The challenge of organizing an extended trip to a remote region for a whole group of foreigners, including one's employer, cannot be exaggerated. Still, flights and hotels were eventually chosen, but other arrangements would, stressfully, have to wait until arrival. As members of the delegation arrived in Beijing, Ben took charge of their passports so that he could go to buy the tickets. Departure for Urumqi, a five-hour flight from Beijing, would take place on Sunday afternoon. As the partners were spread around several hotels, they would all meet at the airport an hour before departure, when Ben could distribute passports and tickets.

It was a fine Sunday morning. With a difficult week ahead, Ben thought he would get some fresh air. He was already packed. He was well practiced, so this took about three minutes. His small hand-carry case (only a novice would entrust his belongings to the People's Airline) contained his current novel plus a spare, so he would not be caught without reading matter. There was also his trusted Walkman to while away the long air and car journeys ahead. His parents had sent out a bundle of requested music tapes with one of the partners, so he was well supplied. He was particularly looking forward to being able to check out the Blue Nile's latest record. His mother, in a vain effort to improve his knowledge of classical music, had included an opera tape— this time of Smetana's "The Bartered Bride". Ben set this aside for some future Sunday morning. His toilet bag included the requisite supply of anti-diarrhoea tablets as well as aspirin for hangovers—it was a heavy-drinking group. All the passports and tickets were in the side pocket. He checked his purse. Yes, there was sufficient cash and a good supply of name cards. There was a stamp-sized picture of Xiao Peng taken in Shanghai. It was inserted in a card holder next to her father's name card.

There was still several hours before he needed to get to the airport. The plane was at three o'clock, so that meant they would meet at two. Even allowing for the poor road and traffic, it was only sixty minutes from the Friendship Hotel to Capital Airport, so he could leave at one. He decided to take a spin on his Iron Anchor. There was a pagoda on the hills behind the Friendship hotel, which he had long meant to check out. Nourished by his daily jam and toast, he wheeled the bike out of the hotel gate, giving a salute to the guard house.

Ben set off, avoiding the roads, preferring to follow tracks through villages and weave between fields. He kept the pagoda ahead of him as a guide to the general direction. Following his Hash experience, he concentrated on the track ahead of his front wheel, swerving to avoid potholes and the track or large stones. The pagoda was a bit further away than he thought, so he speeded up, applying more weight to the pedals and pushing the bike to go faster. That was when he realized he had ridden into the middle of an army camp.

Two guards came running towards him, one waving, and one grasping his rifle. "Xia lai! Xia lai!" Ben screeched to a halt and raised his hands. "Oh, I'm terribly sorry. I didn't realize. I was just out for a spin. I will go back." Ben turned his bike around.

The nearest guard scowled and shouted "Dismount now! Get off your bike. This must be reported."

He gestured to the other soldier to take the bike. Ben reluctantly released it. There was a row of Nissen huts. Ben saw artillery arrayed under camouflage netting. The guard gestured towards the nearest building with his gun. When Ben hesitated, he got a push. "Okay, Okay. Take it easy. I am staying at the Friendship Hotel. I was just out for a bike ride."

The guard kept silent and indicated that Ben should go through the door. It was a spartan office. Someone, clearly senior, sat behind a desk. The guard made his report.

"This foreigner just forced his way through the gates, ignoring all the warning signs. He speaks Chinese. I saw him counting the artillery. He tried to leave, but we stopped him."

"Thank you, Private." The officer dismissed the guards. They did not move far, keen to participate in further interrogation, rather than to return the boredom of guarding a little-used gate. "That will be all, comrades." The guards reluctantly withdrew. The officer turned his attention to Ben. "Passport!" He held out his hand.

"I am terribly sorry, I don't have it. It's at my hotel, the Friendship Hotel. Room 1450. If you can come back with me then…"

"What is your name? What are you doing here? Why did you ignore the No Entry sign on the road?"

"I guess I was concentrating on my bike. The road is a little bumpy. I was on my way to the pagoda."

Ben gestured vaguely in the assumed direction. "I did not realize that this was a…"

"There is a huge warning sign by the road."

"I was riding through the fields, so perhaps…"

"What is your name? Nationality? Passport number?"

Ben proceeded to give him these details, and then his work address.

"I will need to check this out" said the officer sceptically. "Wait here."

Ben glanced down at his watch. It was already 11 a.m. The officer was closing the door.

"Excuse me. I am flying to Urumqi this afternoon, so if… "

This information did not seem improve the officer's demeanor.

"Wait here."

The door closed. Ben heard the lock turn. The only window in the room was above head height. There was a 1983 calendar on the wall, but it was still showing February. The minutes passed slowly. Ben had nothing with him to pass the time. There was the occasional noise of vehicles outside and a muffled voice next door, too low for Ben to make out what was being said. It was now 11:45.. Ben got up and knocked on the door.

"Excuse me! Excuse me! I have a flight this afternoon and…"

The door suddenly opened, and the officer appeared.

"What is it?" he asked, exasperated. "You must be patient and keep quiet. I am handling the matter. I have not yet been able to confirm your information."

"But I have a flight this afternoon at three. I am the guide taking a whole foreign delegation to Xinjiang."

"That has nothing to do with me. Wait here."

The door started to close again.

"Perhaps I can help you. To get the information. If I can use your phone."

Ben had a brainwave and pulled out his wallet. He flourished Mr Peng's name card. It was not what the officer had been expecting or hoping for. Disappointed he accepted the card.

"This is a high-level cadre that I know. If I could just call him then…"

"I'll do it."

Leaving the door open, the officer sat down at his desk to dial. He held the phone to his hear while continuing to stare balefully at Ben. "Wei! Wei!" he shouted down the phone. He explained who he was and, in an imperious manner, that he urgently needed to speak to — he looked more closely at the card — Bureau Chief Peng. There was a pause while the connection was made. Apparently, Peng himself answered. The officer explained the reason for his call: a foreigner on a bike… trespassing on military property… calling himself…claiming that he worked at… There was a short silence before Peng started to reply. The officer, who had been hunched over the desk started to straighten himself. After about a minute he was almost at a salute. "He wants to talk to you."

The officer handed over the receiver.

"Ben? I am sorry about that, but you must be more careful. I think we have set things straight."

"Oh, thank you so much, Mr Peng. That's so kind of you. If in future there's anything I can do for you, then…"

"That's all right. That's all right. Please in future watch where you are going. Please pass the phone back to Officer Zhang." Ben handed over the handset with a smile. Stoney-faced, the officer accepted it, and, after receiving a final bout of instructions, replaced it. No further word was spoken as Ben was escorted out of the compound. The guard gave the officer a quizzical look, but retuned Ben's bike. It was 12.45 p.m. Shit!

He pedalled furiously, glancing regularly at his watch. One glance caused him to miss a pothole. Fortunately, he managed to put his hands out in time. There was a tear in his trousers and grit in his palms, but the bike was Okay. He remounted. Finally, he got back to the hotel, covered in sweat. He dumped his bike and ran up the steps to his room. Arriving there, he briefly considered and rejected the idea of a wash. No time. 1:45 p.m. Shit! Shit! He grabbed his bag and ran to find a taxi.

CHAPTER TWENTY-TWO
What time do you call this?

There is only so fast that a Shanghai-brand taxi can travel, and this was a rusty version that had already seen long service. Emerging from the hotel doors at a jog, Ben had not been in a position to be choosy. His instruction to the driver to drive as fast as possible to the airport was made through gritted teeth. Firstly, there was the question of the variable driving skills of the taxi drivers, often newly arrived in Beijing from the countryside. Ben later learned that in China, learners could pass their test without ever encountering the open road. This explained quite a lot. Then there were the natural obstacles that littered China's roads. He winced as his taxi swerved just in time to miss a donkey cart. A teacher, shepherding her class over a crossing, wisely decided to halt progress as the taxi accelerated towards the crocodile of five-year-olds. When the taxi finally lurched to halt in front of the terminal, Ben was covered with another layer of sweat to add to that derived from his earlier adventures. It was now 2:30 p.m. He dropped a 100 yuan note on the passenger seat and ran for the departure gates.

They were easy to spot—a gaggle of foreigners in front of a deserted departure desk. He was greeted by the chairman of the board, "Where the fuck were you?"

"What time do you call this?" added the chief financial officer.

"Oh, I was so worried you'd have gone," managed Ben.

"Of course we haven't gone. You've got our passports" explained the chairman of the board.

"There is also the small matter of the tickets" added the chief financial officer.

"Have we missed the plane?"

"Apparently not. Lucky you, it's delayed. Sort it out," instructed the chairman, indicating a bored airline employee who was impatiently clicking her nails on the counter.

"Here." Ben thrust a fistful of passports and tickets at the woman, who commenced the laborious task of checking in a number of unsuitably large cases.

"I'm so sorry I'm late."

"What happened?"

"Well, I got arrested."

"What?!" chorused a majority of the board.

"Oh, only temporarily. It was a mistake. They let me go," Ben said, reassuringly. "It's a long story. Oh, thanks."

This last remark was to the woman, who gave him back passports and tickets, with an added layer of boarding cards and news that the plane would soon depart.

"Okay. Let's go."

They headed to the departure lounge.

The People's Airline had not wasted its best plane on the Urumqi route. They were settling into an ancient Tupolev when the head of the Australian branch complained that his seat did not have a safety belt. The hostess, without missing a beat, politely asked him, during take-off, to kindly hold onto the chair in front.

The four engines coughed into life, with a puff of black smoke, and the propellors accelerated to a blur. Ben noticed some worried looks, particularly amongst the wives. This group might be well travelled, but this was straining the risk envelope. As the plane rolled down the runway, the Muslim gentleman sitting next to Ben started to pray audibly and fervently. Around the cabin could be felt a collective will, focused on helping the laboring plane to levitate. It finally took off to a combined sigh of relief.

An hour into the flight, the hostess brought round a small packet of orange juice. "Is that it?" asked the chairman.

"They'll bring round some Chinese tea and coffee later. But I wouldn't touch the coffee," said Ben.

There followed a small, white cardboard box. The delegation moved eagerly to open it. Ben did not, because he knew what was likely to be inside. The chairman removed from the box a bread roll, holding it between finger and thumb. He looked towards Ben. Ben shrugged. The chairman next removed a packet of raisins. Ben shrugged again, this time adding a 'so-so' flick of the hand. The final component of this cornucopia was a hard-boiled egg. The chairman again looked at Ben, who sadly shook his head, "I wouldn't if I were you."

Ben re-found his place in *And Quiet Flows the Don*.

The plane landed at Urumqi only a couple of hours late, which was not bad, considering. Landing proved easier than taking off, but there was still a small smattering of applause as the brakes were released at the end of the runway. Most of the passengers then immediately jumped to their feet and started emptying the overhead lockers as the plane taxied towards its parking spot.

Urumqi airport consisted of a shed. A few chairs had considerately been lined up on the runway in front of the shed, in case anyone felt the need to sit down. Luggage was unloaded onto an open truck, which drove over to the parking area, and started handing down the bags directly to passengers. There were also a few home appliances brought by returning locals or as gifts by visiting relatives. There was also one polystyrene box of crabs, doubtless to impress a desert-bound lover of seafood. All the luggage of Ben's group had, gratifyingly, arrived, and he quickly established that the dusty blue minibus was the one that he had hired, with Driver Ma at its helm. The group and its baggage were bundled aboard and headed for the city.

Chapter Twenty-three
Dishonest

As a city, Urumqi does not have too much to recommend it. It is brutally hot in summer and freezing in winter and regularly subject to sandstorms. The local food is hardly *haute cuisine*, but the Turkish-style lamb kebabs are good, and the pomegranates juicy. Ben left his delegation to the meagre delights of the city as he set about his primary task — organizing suitable mounts for the board's camel race. The chairman had the previous evening proudly showed Ben the silver cup that he had brought out from the UK to award to the winner. Ben's explanation of his task to the hotel's front desk was met with considerable sucking of teeth and shaking of heads. He was eventually assigned a local guide who gloried in the English name of Oscar. With Ma at the wheel and Oscar riding shotgun, the trio headed out in the minibus to find suitable animals.

Thus began a camel odyssey. The pattern was quickly established. Oscar would descend enthusiastically from the minibus. There would be some chat with the camel owner who would then proudly present his herd. Oscar would review the camels, his face gradually becoming longer. Eventually, with a sad shake of his head, he would conclude: "I am sorry, Mr Ben, but these are not honest camels."

"Not honest?"

"Absolutely not."

Honesty, or the more common lack of it, seemed to be the key characteristic of camels. As Oscar chatted to the owners, Ben wandered among the beasts. One spat at him. The smell was unpleasant. Given the weight of some of the board members and the size of the beasts, Ben also started to have doubts about the feasibility of the whole camel-race scenario. As the shadows lengthened, it was discovered that Urumqi could not offer a single honest camel. Ben needed a Plan B—and quick.

The minibus bumped back to town, and a vigorous and wide-ranging discussion ensued. The best alternative seemed to be a horse trek up the mountains by Tianchi, the Heavenly Lake, a couple of hours south of Urumqi. Oscar could definitely arrange this, and Driver Ma knew the route. On his return, Ben sold the new arrangement to his colleagues. The speed and ease with which the new plan was adopted indicated, perhaps, some hidden doubts amongst a number of the party about their camel-riding abilities. Horses were a more familiar challenge.

When the group arrived at the Heavenly Lake, 'horses' turned out to be a misnomer. These were ponies. This was fine with Ben, who had little experience with horse-riding—there would be less far to fall. Each board member was matched to a pony and the trek began. Each pony was led by a young man, who turned out not to be Uyghur but Kyrgyz, another local minority. The escort was important, as the narrow path was bordered by a steep fall on the valley side. Ben gripped the reins tightly and quickly learned not to look down. He kept his eyes on the peak ahead, which he was told was called Bogdapeng. The ponies turned out to be strong and sure-footed—perhaps descendants of the animals that had carried Genghis Khan to his conquests. The trek was broken by a picnic on an elevated grassy bank with a wonderful view down to the lake. There were no further accidents, and, at the end of the afternoon, the group was safely delivered back down to the yurts in which they would be sleeping. Cash in hand, the Kyrgyz men jumped onto their steeds, and with loud whoops, careered off into the distance.

During that evening's meal, Ben endured some mild joshing about his "arrest". A considerable amount of the local "Sinkiang" beer had been consumed when the conversation, no locals being present, turned to international politics. The Chairman leaned towards Ben and pretended to whisper: "An Oxford man like you, studying an exotic language, I am surprised you did not get a tap on the shoulder. You know, from Cheltenham. GCHQ"

Ben had endured enough teasing for one evening. Giving a false grin he asked: "Who says I wasn't? A metal trader free to travel round China would be perfect cover." There was a momentary pause in conversation around the table. Then the CFO let out a huge guffaw: "You? Too much of a loose cannon! Far too likely to go native." Everyone laughed and Ben buried his face in his beer and imagined the CFO riding a dishonest camel.

The camel-race cup could not be presented and sits to this day on a mantelpiece in Oremin's head office. But, overall, the group seemed to enjoy their Xinjiang adventure. Late that night, reluctantly leaving his yurt because of a need to pee, Ben had a lovely view of the full, sad-eyed moon above the peaks of the Tianshan mountains. As he relieved himself, he realized there must have been asparagus chopped into the fried rice.

CHAPTER TWENTY-FOUR
The Request

After returning to Beijing, most of the party flew back to their countries, but the chairman and head of the Australian branch stayed on. This was because they were to participate in a tour by management of the Australian iron-ore client, who were going to visit their largest customers to celebrate the 10th anniversary of supplying China's steel mills.

With only a couple of days back in Beijing, Ben called Xiao Peng and arranged to take her to Beijing's fanciest Western restaurant, which was in the new Jianguo Hotel. In absolute terms, the quality of the cooking was probably not that high, but for a man just back from the Gobi Desert, it was heaven. A nice steak and chips, together with a glass of proper red wine, really hit the spot. Ben could see by the way Xiao Peng toyed with her food that the meal was not to her taste, but she seemed happy with the experience. Towards the end of the meal, she said, "My father mentioned that he is going to call you."

"Sure, that's fine. But I am only going to be in the office a couple of days before I set off with another delegation again. Do you know what it's about?"

Xiao Peng said she did not know. They ordered dessert (crème caramel for Xiao Peng, Eton mess for Ben), and Xiao Peng excused herself to go to the ladies' room. While she was gone, the elderly foreign couple dining at the next table smiled at him. He smiled back. The lady leaned over and said, "Your girlfriend is pretty."

Ben was rather stumped as to how to reply for a moment, but eventually managed, "Oh, thank you."

Ben settled the bill, and Xiao Peng returned from the Ladies. Ben rose and gave the neighboring couple a smile. As they were leaving, he noticed Angela with a group at a table at the back of the restaurant. He had been spotted, so gave a friendly wave. Angela raised a glass in salute.

"Who is that?" asked Xiao Peng.

"She works at the British embassy. I have met her at a couple of embassy events."

Back in the office next day, Ben received the promised phone call: "Oh, Mr Peng. Thank you so much for your help the other day. Without your assistance, I don't know how long I would have been stuck there."

"It was nothing. My pleasure. What I wanted to talk to you about today is something different. We want to buy a crystal puller."

"That's great. We represent an American CZ-method crystal-puller company called EMC."

"I know."

"What model is required?"

"It is a…"

Peng paused, obviously consulting some document: "It is model VS3000. Used to produce Germanium crystals. The customer will be Norinco."

"OK. I will get onto it straight away. I should be able to send you a quote in a couple of days. I am out of town soon, but I have your telex number. There should not be much delay."

Ben was delighted. This would be a feather in his cap. These pieces of equipment were expensive. He included the request in his evening telex back to London. That evening, back in his room, once more packing his bag for the steel tour, he turned up the volume of Elvis Costello's *Shipbuilding* on his tape machine.

CHAPTER TWENTY- FIVE
Steel

The steel tour was a challenge. The companies to be visited were Shougang, Wugang, Angang and Baogang. That is to say, Capital Steel in Beijing, Wuhan Steel in central China, Anshan Iron & Steel up in Manchuria and Baoshan Steel outside Shanghai. That was a lot of travel for one week. At each location, the plant had to be visited and admired. There are few sights more spectacular than a pour of molten steel, sparks flying, or the speed of plate steel being rolled. But observing was hot and grimy work when dressed in an inappropriate suit and tie, balancing borrowed and ill-fitting hard hats while being led along elevated gangways. A bigger challenge, however, was the eating and the drinking. At each location, the Australian iron-ore supplier would lay on a banquet. Chinese etiquette required that the steel company give a return banquet. So that meant two banquets a day for a week. By Friday evening, Ben had never felt so stuffed or hung over.

Apart from the indigestion, the toasts and the repetitive polite conversation, Ben's other abiding memory of this time was watching the whole Australian delegation hunched over a small transistor radio, trying to catch World Service news between storms of interference. The cause was Australia II's challenge for the Admiral's Cup. The Australian yacht, sponsored by leading

Australian businessman Alan Bond, had a chance of becoming the first challenger to take the cup away from the New York Yacht Club since 1851. The race was neck and neck. Much to the delight of the delegation, Australia took the cup 4-3. Alan Bond was toasted in *baijiu* as a national hero. A few years later he went bankrupt and was sent to prison for fraud, but let's not spoil a nice story.

Ben had still not got a reply on Mr Peng's enquiry. Back in the Beijing office, Shirley and Yu had now returned from maternity leave. The atmosphere was distinctly frosty. He tried to explain what had happened regarding the emergency accommodation, he apologized, but none of it seemed to do any good. Ben did not want to discuss Mr Peng's inquiry with Shirley or Yu, partly because it was his win and partly because it was an EMC engineer who had slept in their bed. He decided to follow up the matter directly with a call to Cameron, the head of the equipment division back in London.

"I'm sorry we didn't get back to you. We cannot supply that model to China."

"What do you mean?"

"That model is restricted under the Bureau of Industrial Security's ECCN restrictions. It stands for Export Control Classification Number. That model has military applications. Chips for missiles, apparently. Sorry."

"So what shall I tell them?"

"That we are, unfortunately, unable to supply them with this model. There are of course older models with lower specifications..."

Shirley, who had been listening to the conversation, shook her head. "I could have told you that model is banned."

Disappointed, Ben waited until Shirley had left the office — earlier than usual because of the baby — to call Mr Peng to relay the bad news. Mr Peng's reaction was not what he had expected. "Oh, that's not a problem. It is easy to find a way around the US sanctions."

"Sorry? What do you mean? How?"

"Well, you can ship the model we need, but document it as an older model. Or you can say you are supplying it to a customer in another country — Indonesia is acceptable, I believe — then ship it from there to China. Or you can supply the older model, then when the engineer comes to install the machine, he hand-carries with him the key components from the new model to upgrade the one already supplied. You see, there are all sorts of ways. You have been helpful in the past, with the cobalt and all. Given your affection for my daughter, you feel almost like family. I am sure you will work it out. Call me when you have."

The line went dead. Ben sat silently at his desk for a while, trying to work out what had just happened.

Ben looked at his watch — the London office should be in by now. He called Cameron. He had just started to relay Mr Peng's response when Cameron interrupted him, "It would be better to discuss this face to face. I am coming out to Hong Kong next week."

"I am due some R&R and need to renew my visa. I can meet you there."

A time and place was agreed.

Before he left, Ben called Xiao Peng, to let her know he would be away for a few days and see if she wanted him to bring anything back from Hong Kong.

"My father says you are doing something for him."

"Well, trying to."

"He was a bit vague. What is it? It is like the hero being set a series of tasks to win a maiden's hand?"

She giggled.

CHAPTER TWENTY-SIX
Diary

9/10/83

I don't know what more I can do. I have given enough hints, but he does nothing. Perhaps I have got it wrong. Maybe he already has a girlfriend back home. Perhaps the blond girl I saw him wave to. I think I could have talked my father round. I can see the matter has been discussed, as my mother has stepped up her campaign to introduce me to a suitably qualified local boy. Anyway, he is lucky enough to have two daughters. My sister can give him the nice fat Chinese grandson he wants, and leave me to make my own way and see the world. Mother can sense my frustration. She is getting smarter; her latest candidate is a "sea turtle" who has returned with a degree from Chicago.

CHAPTER TWENTY-SEVEN
R&R

A sea eagle flew beneath him, turning lazy circles over the wooded slopes below. Further out, a stand of skyscrapers marched down to the harbor. Ben was staying in the Mid-Levels apartment of a college friend who had joined the Hong Kong police force. His friend had gone off to work early, and Ben's meeting with Cameron was not until late afternoon, so for now he had nothing better to do than sit on the balcony of the high-rise apartment block, with a cold beer and *The Master and Margarita*, watching the eagles and the Peak Tram crawl up the mountain like a green caterpillar. He had already been to China Travel's office in Central yesterday to sort out his visa. He had ticked off two of the three foodstuffs vital to any break from China — a glass of decent red wine and a bar of proper dark chocolate. Only the consumption of an Indian curry remained, and he was booked for tiffin at the Hilton later.

Ben's arrival in Hong Kong this time had been particularly exciting. His friendship with the Beijing rep for British Airways meant that he got to sit in the cockpit for the landing at Kai Tak airport. When he was first invited into the cabin, the atmosphere was relaxed; the captain and co-pilot were joking around. But as the approach started there was a distinct change in attitude.

Everyone buckled in. The navigator started to call out wind-speed. The 747 suddenly banked to the left. Ben could tell the color of the underpants which a man was hanging on his roof's laundry line. He hoped the runway would be appearing soon. The plane cleared the perimeter fence by what seemed like a few feet and the wheels hit the deck. Ben knew the short runway ended in Hong Kong harbor, so found himself unconsciously pressing down his right foot on an imaginary brake. He could feel the general sense of relief once the brake could be eased and the flaps returned to normal position. The cabin door opened to a gust of fetid harbor air.

Ben enjoyed his short visits to Hong Kong, this China-but-not-China. The gleaming malls of Wanchai, full of artfully presented fashions, were such a contrast to the fusty, ill-stocked department stores in Beijing, where the most frequently uttered phrase was *meiyou* ("We haven't got it."). It is not that Ben bought anything, but the window-shopping was amusing, watching the over-dressed *tuitai* graze on displays like exotic tropical fish on a coral reef. There was a bookstore that he always visited to re-stock. Its selection of English-language books was limited, mostly consisting of bestsellers and self-help books about how to become a millionaire, but it was better than nothing.

There remained strange remnants of Empire. On his previous visit, he had been invited for lunch at the Hong Kong Club. He was forced to borrow a striped tie from reception. A lounge was stocked with old copies of the *Spectator*. The food was dire. Ben was not a public schoolboy, but he recognized the selection of nursery foods of the meat-and-two-veg and suet-pudding-with-custard variety, designed to feed the nostalgia of earlier homesick servants of Empire. It was in another Imperial relic that Ben met Cameron that evening—the Captain's Bar at the Mandarin. Cameron, the old China hand, showed Ben how beer could be ordered in pewter jugs (this did not improve the taste, but Ben was too polite to say anything). A selection of crisps and nuts was provided gratis. On his visit to the WC, Ben was startled, after a cursory washing of his hands, to be presented with a freshly pressed serviette by a butler. Clearly a tip was expected. Ben fumbled in his purse for an amount that might be appropriate. Tipping was frowned upon on the Mainland, so he was out of practice.

Cameron chatted about developments in the London office, before pointedly asking how Ben was getting on with Shirley and Yu. Clearly critical reports had got back to him. There were also a couple of jokes about Ben's problematic relationship with camels and the People's Liberation Army. It was twenty minutes before Ben could raise the issue of Mr Peng's order. Cameron's equipment-agency division was a poor relative to the metal-trading department, so he was in need of the business, but it was also clear that nothing could be done, "For commodities, it is easier to get around sanctions. We can act as principal, both as buyer and seller, and it is not difficult to re-route a cargo. For advanced equipment, it is more difficult. I discussed the matter with the CEO of EMC. It's too dangerous for them to fall afoul of the US authorities. It's just not worth the risk. Do you want another beer?"

That was it.

CHAPTER TWENTY-EIGHT
Tough Call

Back in Beijing, the temperature was cooler both outside and inside the office. Shirley asked how Ben had enjoyed his holiday, and how the meeting with Cameron had gone. Ben did not rise to the bait but gave a neutral answer. He had decided just to keep his head down and get on with the job. He was nervous about the call he had to make to Mr Peng. He called when his colleagues were out on a client visit. The secretary put him through.

"Wei!"

"Hello, Mr Peng. It's me. Ben. I am calling to give you an update on the crystal puller. It seems difficult to ship the model you want to China. US restrictions."

"Yes." Ben waited for Mr Peng to continue, but there was only silence.

"So my company says it cannot supply this particular model to you."

"How disappointing."

There was a further silence. Ben could not end the conversation like this, in failure. He had a brainwave.

"Let me call the company directly."

He still had the name card of the ECM engineer, Jim, who he had put up in Yu and Shirley's bed. "I will do my best. I will let you know if there is any progress." The Chinese version of this sentence sounded less positive than this English translation. Chinese is a good language in which to be vague, with its lack of tenses and relaxed use of the personal pronoun.

"I am counting on you."

The receiver was replaced. Xiao Peng's father was clearly not a man for small talk.

Calling ECM would be tricky given the sixteen-hour time difference with San Francisco. If he booked a call with his hotel reception for seven the next morning, that should catch Jim in the office the previous afternoon. Ben was ready the next morning, fortified only by Chinese tea and a digestive biscuit from an emergency packet he had stashed. The phone rang and the receptionist said she would put him through. There was the normal clicking on the phone; Ben imagined someone somewhere pressing a recorder button. After several rings, an American voice answered faintly.

"Hello. Is that ECM? I am looking for Mr Jim Fisher?"

Ben found himself shouting, the result of getting used to the Chinese telephone system.

"Hi? Jim Fisher speaking."

"Hello, this is Ben. From Beijing. You know, from Oremin."

"Oh, yes Ben. How are you?"

"Fine, fine. I have a couple of questions about ECM equipment. Do you have a moment now?"

"Sure. How can I help you?"

"Well, it's about the difference between the CZ4000 model, which you installed when you last came to China, and the CZ6000."

"We don't supply the CZ6000 to China."

"Yes, I know. But I have some questions from clients and

97

would like to check them with you."

There followed a rather tortuous conversation where Ben tried to find out, without this appearing to be his intention, whether it was possible to upgrade a CZ4000 to a CZ6000 by importing some specific additional parts. The poor quality of the phone line, which required the conversation to be carried out at high volume, worked against such subtlety. It seemed to revolve around pulling head speed, yield and micro-defects.

"So, do you think a CZ4000 could be upgraded by bringing in a new pulling head and ancillary parts? And, if so, what would be the cost?"

"I will have to check and get back to you."

"That's great."

Ben was effusive in his thanks. "I'll talk to you soon." Ben went downstairs for, he thought, some well-earned coffee and toast, both of which suffered from more than micro-defects.

Chapter Twenty-nine

Oz

A blast of heat stopped him at the top of the airplane's steps, and he looked out at a landscape that resembled Mars. As the small private jet was taxiing to a halt, there had been a thud. The pilot came on the speaker to apologize, in a strong Australian accent, saying, "We've just rolled over a Goanna". Acting as Strine-to-Chinese translator, Ben explained to the delegation from Baoshan Iron & Steel that the bump had been one of the local lizards, which used the mine's airstrip to sun themselves.

Ben was accompanying the Chinese mission on a visit to one of the world's largest iron ore mines in Australia's Northwest. Shirley and Yu had been happy to allot the task to Ben who, given the tensions in the Beijing office, had been just as happy to accept. When the pilot informed them the temperature at Marble Bar was forty degrees Celsius, Ben wondered whether he should have been quite so eager. There had first been a long flight from China down to Perth and then a transfer on this small jet up to the mines.

The view from the top of the steps revealed no evidence of human habitation. The delegation, used to the jostling, crowded streets of Shanghai, were clearly unnerved as they de-planed. Dust the color of rust instantly coated their shoes as they shuffled to the waiting minibus.

The head of the Australian office, Ron, greeted the delegation. While shaking hands with the delegation leader, he waved away circling flies. "West Australian salute!" he joked. Ben struggled to translate. Accommodation was in bungalows at the mine. Once the delegation had been fed, watered and shown to their respective rooms, the head of the Australian office, Ron, with whom Ben was sharing a room, had, like a magician, produced two cold beers from a fridge in the kitchenette. Sitting at a Formica table, they clinked cans. "Welcome to Australia! What do you think of it so far?"

"Well, Perth seemed nice. Green, and well laid out. Here seems more... challenging."

"Yes, it's not a spot where many want to stay for too long. But the wages are good, and the R&R breaks frequent. It's not that different from the Gobi Desert."

He smiled. "Perhaps we should have come here for our camel racing."

He paused and took another sip of beer. "What did you do to piss Cameron off?"

"Did I?"

"I had a call with him yesterday, and he seemed unhappy. Something about calling a company direct when he had already told you they could not ship to China."

"Oh, I see."

Ben's stomach churned. Another black mark against his name. "It was about importing some semiconductor equipment, from ECM. There is a customer who is keen, but it seems US sanctions are going to prevent it. It would have been a nice contract."

On the second beer, Ben could not help but complain about the atmosphere in the Beijing office. Ron provided a sympathetic ear. Once the beers were finished, the men took turns to use the bathroom, then retired to bed. Ron turned out to have the loudest snore Ben had ever heard. The windowpanes vibrated. Resigning himself to a sleepless night, Ben fished the Walkman from his bag and inserted earbuds.

Breakfast next morning was in the workers' canteen. There was a long self-service buffet. Ben politely gave the delegation leader a plate and told him to serve himself first. The leader proceeded to pile his plate with cornflakes, a grilled tomato, a sausage, two slices of bacon and some baked beans. After a moment's hesitation, he added a scoop of fruit salad. The rest of the delegation followed their leader's example, then carefully carried their pyramids of breakfast food back to a long table, where they proceeded to clean their plates to the last cornflake, with expressions of satisfaction.

Suitably fortified, the team headed for the huge open-cut mine. The company had arranged for the delegation to attend a blasting, which sounded exciting. The minibus bumped up a red dirt track, weaving skilfully between enormous oncoming trucks loaded with ore. On reaching an elevated ledge, the team got off and were told to watch the other side of the valley. "Are you ready?"

Ben tensed and covered his ears. For a moment, nothing happened. Then, in the far distance, a series of small puffs of smoke flowered in the silence.

"Is that it?" thought Ben, disappointed. A moment later, he was hit by the sonic boom. To a man, the team flinched and swayed backwards.

The afternoon's entertainment was a helicopter flight over the port of Dampier. It was the first time that Ben had been on a helicopter, and he was impressed by the noise, even through the headphones they had all been given. Down below, a series of conveyor belts filled huge Capesize ore carriers with iron ore for the China market. The helicopter banked over the harbor, following one ship that was heading out. The headphones were tuned to the ship's communication channel. To the Chinese speakers' embarrassment, they were listening in to a discussion about laundry. The leader shook his head and placed a finger to his lips.

Ben woke to the sparkle of water reflecting on his bedroom ceiling. He was now in Sydney, and the windows gave a magnificent view of the Harbor Bridge. After seeing the delegation off on their flight back to China, Ben got to spend some time in the Sydney office. There was a meeting with the rest of the local team, and discussions about how the Australian business could be expanded beyond its current reliance on the trading of a limited number of minerals. But the star was the city itself. Ben had been accommodated at a serviced apartment on Harbor Point, right down by the water. He journeyed to the office by ferry across the bay—surely one of the world's best commutes. At dinner, the seafood was fresh, and mercifully free of sea slugs. The local Chardonnay was also a distinct improvement on torture by *baijiu*. As he was raving about it, Ron said, "Well, if you ever want a job down here, let me know."

It was tempting. He'd bought a postcard of Sydney for Xiao Peng. He imagined standing together with her by the harbor's edge. After a moment's consideration, he decided to mail it in an envelope—probably safer that way. He would probably beat the postcard back to Beijing, but it showed he was thinking of her.

He flew back to China via Hong Kong to renew his visa. As he queued with his documents in hand, there was a nagging worry that his issues in China might cause a problem with his visa. But the mountains are high and the emperor far away, as the saying goes, and his passport was stamped without incident.

His room at the Friendship Hotel was as he had left it. It was strange how somewhere so alien could come to smell of home. It was probably just the type of furniture polish they used. An aid parcel had arrived from England, so his music library had been expanded with tapes of music by Jethro Tull and Tears for Fears, together with his mother's recording of Radio 1's Top 40 radio show. In the office, little had changed—nothing was, it seems, forgiven or forgotten. There was almost no conversation that was not directly work-related. The silences during the morning and evening lift to and from the office became uncomfortable. Ben found excuses to make his own way to work—sometimes on his bike, saying that he needed more exercise though, in truth, the journey was rather sweaty and not altogether safe. Coming back from lunch one day, dawdling on the stairs, he overhead Yu and Shirley discussing recruitment. The conversation took place in Cantonese, and he only caught a few phrases, so it might have been about office expansion, but it sounded more like replacement.

Ben left several messages for Xiao Peng, but his calls were not returned. He supposed that she might be out of town or busy with delegations.

CHAPTER THIRTY-ONE
The Match

Given Xiao Peng's absence, and the frostiness at the office, Ben was an early and enthusiastic participant in TGIF. This week all the talk was of the week-end's main event—a football match between Watford and the Chinese national team. Watford were not one of England's more fashionable sides, but someone on the marketing team had the bright idea to use a pre-season tour to spread the word in Asia. China did not even have a professional football league, or, given the notable absence of large urban green spaces for kicking a ball around, much grass-roots participation or interest—the suitably contained exercise of Table Tennis was the national sport and Ben had long learned to avoid ping pong games with Chinese, to avoid humiliation. But a national soccer team had been rounded up, and it sounded like it might be a laugh, so Ben found a ticket and went along.

Attendance at the Worker's Stadium was thin. The local crowd, some of whom seemed to have been bussed in to make up the numbers, were not sure what to make of the event. The confusion was clearly shared by the organizers who had, charmingly, printed on the admission tickets "Applaud both sides". The foreign crowd, whilst boasting few Watford supporters, did their best to fill the vacuum with some shouting and chanting. The gap between the skills of the two sides was soon evident. Watford's forward line was led by a tall black striker called Luther Blissett. The Chinese crowd soon came to understand that when he got the ball, the Chinese team were in trouble, so his every touch started to be met with an anticipatory "oooow".

Goals soon followed. For the opening one, the unfortunate Chinese goalkeeper raced out to punch a high ball, missed it completely, and it rolled into the net. He was immediately substituted. He trudged off the field with his head hung low. After his exit down the tunnel, Ben expected a shot to be heard from behind the stands.

After the final whistle, as the ironic applause for all-conquering Watford team faded, Ben heard his name called. A man in a suit was making his way through the departing crowd "You are Ben." It was a statement more than a question. The accent was American.

"Yes" admitted Ben "I am sorry I don't…"

I am Chris. Chris Fowlds. From the U.S. Embassy. I have seen you at one of the TGIFs"

"That's possible"

"And your name came up recently at work. You act as an agent for some U.S. equipment companies here, including EMC."

"Yes, that's right. I would be happy to have a chat with you, but I am so sorry, I need to rush off for a meeting now. Perhaps at the next TGIF?" Ben did not wait for an answer but pushed his way out through the crowd. As he passed the turnstiles, Ben was focussed on a more permanent exit. Facing pressure from the weapons ministry in China was bad enough. Now he seemed to be in the cross-hairs of the U.S. authorities as well. If he were suddenly to disappear, who would campaign for his return. His company would not want endanger their whole business in

China for some "loose cannon". Would the "cocktail boys" of the British embassy, true allies of the U.S., make anything more than a polite enquiry? Who would pay any attention to his elderly parents in Leeds or sister in Croydon? Ben mentally calculated the time difference between Beijing and Sydney. He would call Ron first thing Monday morning about his job offer.

CHAPTER

CHAPTER THIRTY-TWO
Under the Bridge

This time Xiao Peng responded almost immediately to his message. Probably because it had sounded more urgent. She had fixed a meeting at the same time and place as their first assignation. At this season, there was a still a little color left in the park. A few late chrysanthemums valiantly held on against a sharp autumnal breeze. The surface of the lake was still occasionally disturbed by fish twisting below.

After fifteen minutes, he had completed a thorough survey of the surroundings. A woman, well wrapped in a padded blue jacket, swept the path around the lake, occasionally stooping to capture a piece of litter and deposit it into the cart she pushed. The second time she passed, she gave Ben a funny look. He pretended to be engaged in some calisthenics, propping up his foot on the top of a fence and leaning forward to stretch his muscles, as he had seen done. The cleaner looked unconvinced. Ben did a few jumping jacks. He walked backwards for a stretch, another park favorite, taking care not to fall into the lake. The park was becoming busier, but there was still no sign of Xiao Peng. He looked at his watch again and decided to give her another ten minutes. He gave a smile to the cleaner, who scowled back and returned to her Sisyphean task.

A photographer and soon-to-be-married couple had come to the lake to take some photos for the wedding album. Having doffed her thick jacket, the bride-to-be was shivering. Several dramatic poses were struck in swift succession, the photographer working quickly to ward off hypothermia. Walking up behind the couple, Ben could see that the bride's dress did not fit, but was temporarily held together at the back with a couple of safety pins. Ben kicked a stone into the lake, gave a final glance at his watch and said under his breath "When the hope-hour stroked its sum, she did not come."

He turned to find his bicycle. He had got the message. He had thought Xiao Peng's feelings to be genuine, but maybe she had been working with her father all the time? Perhaps he was just the convenient idiot, a foreigner who could be manipulated to bring in contraband and boost family finances.

Chapter Thirty-three

Exit

Ron seemed pleased to receive Ben's call. If he was surprised by the urgency of Ben's request, he did not question it. Ben's exit from Beijing, and transfer to the Sydney office was negotiated. Yu and Shirley were hardly going to fight to retain him, once they had been assured that a new assistant would be hired asap.

Ben's worry now was that he would be prevented from leaving. On his last afternoon in the office, Ben told Shirley that he was leaving on the Monday plane when he had actually booked the Saturday flight. With so many loose ends of business to be swiftly tied, he was still cleaning up his room on the last morning. Photos and documents were all swept into the side-pocket of his suitcase. He had decided to donate his beloved boombox and many of his books, including a well-thumbed *500 Useful Business Phrases in Chinese*, to his, as yet, un-named successor.

This time he left for the airport unusually early. The office would settle his hotel bill, and his luggage was the same he always travelled with, so he was able to make a surreptitious departure. The Shanghai taxi made its way to the airport with only the normal number of near-misses. The Qantas plan had not yet arrived but was expected. His booking was in order, and a boarding card for a window seat issued. He dropped his bags and used a ledge for the tedious task of filling in his departure card and readied his duplicated customs declaration. He joined the queue to pre-check his documents. There was no man in dark glasses and ill-fitting suit standing behind the girl who stamped his boarding card. At the emigration counter he gave his most winning smile to the glum official, who applied one of the large, passport-filling exit visas. It was only at customs that the problem occurred.

"Where is the musical instrument?"

"Pardon?"

"The musical instrument which you declared on your customs form when entering the country." The official gestured pointed to the appropriate spot on the form. The damned boombox.

"Oh, that was a tape machine. It broke. I threw it away." The official gave Ben a look of deep suspicion, that mingled with a clear desire to avoid an argument with a foreigner when a tea break was due. The official gestured for Ben to proceed.

The long wait at the departure gate was not a peaceful one. Ben found he had read the same page of "Barnaby Rudge" three times. Ben normally avoided the scrum that formed when boarding was announced, but this time he found himself towards the front of the queue, having spotted the staff's preparations. At the bottom of the boarding bridge his boarding card was checked for the fifth time. The normal long-haul plane stink of overcooked food, old farts and cleaning fluid this time smelt of freedom. He stowed his luggage and took his window seat. 31A. The flight was pretty empty. Maybe he would be able to get some sleep later. It was only when the boarding gate was pushed away that he realized he had been holding his breath.

CHAPTER THIRTY-FOUR
Epilogue

It was only a month later, when he had moved into rented accommodation in Neutral Bay Sydney and was finally sorting out his goods, that he came across an unopened letter from Xiao Peng. The letter was formed in characters that looked as though written by someone younger, but still impressive given she was writing in a foreign language. The letter ended "I am sorry I did not come that day. I tried to talk my father round, but he is a stubborn man. I did love you, you know, Big Stupid, and not just for the passport. Xiao Peng xox".

Ben met Xiao Peng one more time. It was more than twenty years later, and a brave new century had dawned. Her picture had come up on his Facebook page as "Somone you may know". He had clicked on the "Add Friend" button which, to his surprise, had been accepted. It was difficult to get much information from her Facebook page, but the very fact that she had one must mean she spent time outside the 'Great Fire Wall' of China. On his next trip up from Sydney, he sent a message: *Will be back in Beijing in mid-September. Will you be around?*

They arranged to meet, perhaps for old times' sake, in a park. This time it was at Beihai. In a once low-rise city now transformed by skyscrapers and ring-roads, this park in the heart of old Beijing was little changed. Ben had once hosted a business dinner here at a restaurant run by a family which, allegedly, had cooked for the Dowager Empress. Ben was worried that he would not recognize her among the weekend crowds. In the event she was not difficult to spot. She was a little stouter, but still had the same smile, topped by the beauty spot. In an act of folly only partly explained by the unusually smog-free day, Ben suggested they hire a pedalo in the shape of a swan. She laughed.

Out on the lake, whilst pedalling, they caught up. She had built up her own trading business — something to do with textile quotas. It sounded successful and involved travel to the US from time to time. She was married to a man who had studied abroad. She brought out some photos. There were not one but two teenage children. She hoped to send them to study abroad — Chicago was mentioned — thus fulfilling her own dream of foreign study by proxy. Their conversation was pleasant, but only floated over the surface of things. He asked after her father — now long retired, but still playing chess. He found he could not ask the real question. That boat had long sailed. She had some of the same mannerisms he remembered — she still rubbed her hands together when excited. They parted amicably, but no promises were made to keep in touch.

Ben wondered what an alternative future might have looked like, had he been more... persistent.

About The Author

Born in Yorkshire, Chris has spent over 30 years working in Asia. He studied Chinese at Oxford University and Japanese at Sheffield. After graduation, he sold soap in Newcastle, before moving to China with a metal trading company in 1983. He has subsequently worked in finance in Tokyo, Taipei, Edinburgh and Hong Kong and planted a vineyard, with Scottish castle in Shandong. This experience was described in his earlier memoir *A Decent Bottle of Wine* in China (Earnshaw Books, 2015). His play about the burning of the Summer Palace, Before the Wall, was performed at the National Museum of Scotland in 2019. Chris is married with four children.